The Rodeo Ranch

Book 5 Hidden Valley Series

_____

Penny Heggie Austin

The Rodeo Ranch

ISBN (978-1-09834-394-1)

Printed in USA by 48HrBooks (www.48HrBooks.com)

This book is dedicated to my very special sisters in Christ who not only helped edit my books, but also encouraged me over the years and have always been with me when I needed them most.

God's blessings to you all. You are and always will be precious to me.

Penny Heggie Austin

We need to put all our faith in our Father. No matter what has happened in the past. Remember God alone has a plan for us.

You can also be assured that He alone puts the right people at the right time into our life.

As you read this book, "The Rodeo Ranch" you will realize how all these things are true.

Thank you, Miss Penny for bringing these wonderful truths to us in your books.

Claire Clutts,
Florida

Trust in the Lord with all your Heart, and do not lean on your own understanding. In all ways acknowledge Him and He will make straight your paths.

Proverbs: 3: 5-6

My Lord has held my hand through so many times of pain and heartache. I write my books in hopes of helping other know that he is always there for them also. If only a few people realize what a wonderful Savior we have it is always worth it. Always place your faith and trust in Him.

Penny Heggie Austin

Chapter One

Jackson was sitting in his office looking at the outside arena. He could see her out there, working with the girls. Teaching them barrel racing skills. He started thinking back to what brought him to this point. The more he knows her the way she is now, the more he loves her. If he lets her in his life again, she could hurt him even worse than before. "Lord help me. I don't know what you want of me. Let me know what your plans are for us. I am willing to listen. I love the work we are doing here and she is a big part of it. Please give me strength. Amen" He thought back to his last night at the rodeo, his last ride. He was retiring. He stayed at the rodeo longer than he planned in hopes she might show up. He knew he was being foolish. She left him without a word. It had been four years. He thought it was time to give up.

Then he remembered the first time he saw her. She was in the arena working the barrels. She was beautiful and she and her horse worked as one. That was six years ago. He fell head over heels in love with her. She was so young though. He was six years older than she. He took his time to get to know her. He thought she'd gotten to know him. They seemed to really love each other and then the night he was going to propose she left without finishing her last run. She was in line to win the Nationals, but just disappeared.

Why he was thinking about her after all these years. He knew he never got over her and probably never would unless he found out what happened.

Then Jackson's brother Jeff called him. Jeff was getting married, and wanted him to be his best man. He left for Virginia right after the rodeo. Jeff also said he found their baby sister Meredith, who disappeared after she graduated high school. He couldn't wait to get there and see everyone.

He'd looked up the town where Jeff lived and thought maybe it would be a good place to settle down.

When the buzzer went off. The ride was over. The announcer said, "Folks you have seen a championship ride. Rodeo is not going to be the same without Jackson Barnes. Jackson, we are going to miss you around here."

Jackson waved to the audience and left the arena. He wanted to get away before the newspapers started swarming him.

He went to the stables, loaded his horses and left the fair grounds for the last time. He was a little sad, but knew it was time.

Two hours down the road, Jackson pulled into an RV park catering to horse people. He took care of his horses and went to bed. He needed to get some rest before he drove the last eight hours to his brother's home in Hidden Valley, Virginia.

The next morning, he called Jeff and said he would be there that evening.

He told Jeff he would need to find a place to board his horses.

Jeff said not to worry. He knew of a place where he could board them until he found a place to live."

When he started down the road again, his mind went back to Barbara. Why did he keep thinking about her after all these years? He asked the Lord why he kept bringing her back into his mind.

Jackson learned to be satisfied with his life. It'd been a good one. He became a preacher and held services for years at the rodeos. He won several Championships. He saved enough money to buy his ranch and livestock. So why was he thinking of her? Why was he thinking back to what should have been?

He thought okay Lord, I guess you will tell me why this is happening, when you are ready. Just make it soon or I will think I've gone crazy.

Jackson stopped a couple of times on the way to Jeff's to exercise his horses. When he got to Hidden Valley, it was early evening. He started looking for Jeff's house. When he found the beautiful Victorian home, he was amazed. He pulled to the side of the road and turned on his running lights. He looked toward the house and saw a beautiful woman with blond hair come out of the house. He knew she was his future sister-in-law. He thought, his brother was a very lucky man.

She waved and walked down to meet him. She gave him a hug and said she was glad he got there alright.

He told her he would find someplace for his horses and come back later. It looks like they had company. He didn't want to interrupt.

Just then Jeff came around the house and when Jackson looked up, he saw Meredith with him. She ran into his arms and started crying. He held her and told her how happy he was to see her.

He told her that he thought he saw her in Palestine at the rodeo, but by the time he could get out there she was gone.

She told him she knew he was riding. She didn't think he would want to see her after what she did, so she left when he finished his ride".

He told her they were all worried about her. They always wanted her to come home.

Jeff told him to come to the back of the house and get something to eat. Then they would get his horses taken care of.

Jeff took him around to meet everyone. He introduced him to Hank, Tom and Bill and their wives. Hank asked him how many horses he needed a place for. Jackson said he had four he needs to board until he can find a ranch to buy.

Hank told him he knew of a ranch for sale with 1,000 acres, a beautiful home, and barn. It had a bunk house and two stables.

Jackson told him he would love to see it.

Hank said they would take his horses out to his ranch as soon as he'd eaten. He would take him to see the ranch the next day. The owner's wife just died and he wanted to sell it as soon as he could.

He asked Hank if he could park his RV at his ranch for right now.

Hank said it would be fine. He had plenty of room.

Jackson went to eat. When he finished eating Hank said they would be back for dessert. He and Jackson left to go out to the estate.

Tyler, Zack, and the Price boys all wanted to go with them so Jackson let them ride in the motorhome.

Jackson thought he was going to enjoy getting to know all of these people. This was just what he'd been wanting. To be a part of a family again.

When they pulled up to the stable a dark-haired woman was coming out of the stables. Jackson just stared for a minute and then thought it couldn't be, but it was, it was Barbara. He asked God what He was doing to him?

When he got out of the RV Hank called her over to where they were to introduce him. Barbara just looked at him, then asked how he was doing. He swallowed and said he was fine.

Hank looked at the two of them and asked if they knew each other. Jackson said they met at the rodeo. If she wanted to tell him more it was up to her. Right then, his insides were turning over and he just wanted to get the horses taken care of and get away from there.

Hank asked Barbara if she wanted to go back to Jeff's with them.

She said she would come later to bring the little ones back and get them ready for bed.

When they headed back to Jeff's, Jackson asked, why she was coming after the children?

He told him she is their Nanny.

He thought to himself this was why God put her in his mind so much. He asked God what he expect from him.

Jackson knew he didn't want to lose this chance to be with his family or buy the ranch. He guessed he would just have to make sure he didn't run into her often. He thought he could handle it when he did. He could do it with God's help.

The next morning, Hank come out to get Jackson. He said they would go look at the ranch he told him about.

He told Hank he appreciated what he was doing for him. He really did not expect to find something this fast. This is what he'd been working for. He had saved most of his earnings for this.

Jackson loved the ranch and bought it. He had a lot of plans for it. He planned to raise rodeo livestock. He wanted to still be involved with the rodeo. He didn't want to compete anymore. That was a year ago and he still hadn't bought any livestock.

He and Cal, his brother, started the Youth Camp almost a year ago, with the help of family and friends. Barbara was helping there too. She was teaching barrel racing. They'd gone from weekend camps to a summer camp and now while school was on, they'd be back to the weekend camps.

They built the ranch into a good place for the kids. Now he needed to take time to build up his rodeo livestock. He let his dream slide while they were concentrating on the Youth Camp.

He and Jeff were taking turns preaching at the Spanish Church. He also preached for Pastor Nate when he needed time off. His dream was set aside. He still wanted to raise rodeo livestock. He needed the income to keep the ranch running.

His mind came back to the present and he realized he was still watching her through the window. She looked over at him. She smiled and his heart skipped a beat. He really needed to get away from here for a few days. He decided to go look at some livestock, he'd found for sale.

He called the ranch in West Virginia where he'd seen the ad. He planned with the owner to be there in two days. It gave him time to pull the cattle trailer there and plan for the ranch while he is gone.

He went out to talk to Cal and George Turner his ranch hand. He told them of his plans. Cal told him they could take care of things there. Cal asked him if he was okay. He looked tired.

I just need to get away for a while. This gives me the chance to do it. I shouldn't be gone more than a few days if you think you can take care of everything here.

"We can handle it okay. You need to spend this time to make some decisions about your life. You two can't keep going like this. You need to talk to her and find out why she left and put it behind you. You both love each other everyone can see it."

"It is one of the reasons I have to get away for a while. I need to get my mind and heart straight. I will try to talk to her when I get back."

"Okay, I won't say anymore. You have to do what you think is best. Just pray hard about it while you are away."

He went over to the outdoor arena. "Barbara, I need to speak to you in the office when you are done".

"I'll be there in about a half-hour. I need to take care of the horses first."

While Barbara was taking care of the horses, she wondered what Jackson wanted to talk about. He never asked to talk to her in private. Maybe he was going to tell her he wants her to leave the ranch. She hoped not. She didn't think she could stand not seeing him every day. She knew she would miss working with the children.

He knew she was there before she knocked. He could always feel her presence. He told her to come in.

"Jackson, is something wrong?"

"Nothing is wrong, I just need to ask you a question. I know you were taking accounting in college and I wondered if I could hire you to bring the Camp books up to date for me. I need to have a meeting with Hank and the other investors and let them know how things stand."

"Jackson, I would love to do it for you. I can work on them while the little ones are in pre-school. Shane is in first-grade now so he will be gone all day. Would it work out okay for you?"

"Great, I will be leaving tomorrow for a few days. I need to go check on some livestock for the ranch. You can use the office. I'll leave everything on my desk and the password for the computer. I will pay you for the work of course."

"Jackson, you don't have to pay me. I want to help the camp any way I can."

She was disappointed he was going to be gone, but maybe it was best. She didn't know if she could concentrate with him there.

"Barbara, don't you think it is about time we talked? I need you to tell me why you left. I need to have closure. If I did something, I need to know it. I loved you and planned on asking you to marry me and all of a sudden you were gone."

"Jackson, it was nothing you did. I was very unsure of myself. We will talk when you get back and I will try to explain as best I can. I did love you though."

"Okay, we will leave it for right now. I should be back in a few days and then we will talk. Thank you for doing this for me."

When Jackson went to bed, he asked God to help him listen to Barbara without the pain he felt all these years and help him understand and show compassion and love.

Jackson left early the next morning for West Virginia to look at the livestock. The owner told him he was retiring and wanted to sell all the animals. He told Jackson he knew of him and would make him a good deal if he would take everything.

Jackson knew the ranch where he was going. He'd ridden some of its bulls and broncs. He knew they were the best Rodeo livestock in the country. He also knew the ranch foreman. He was usually the one who came with the livestock to the rodeo. He had never met the owner.

He pulled up to the ranch around five in the evening. The Foreman, Davis Lightfoot told him the owner wanted him to stay at the ranch while they did their business. Jackson thanked him and said he appreciated it.

Jasper, the owner of the ranch, saw him pull up the lane and came out to meet him. He introduced himself and told Jackson to come in and have a drink with him. Jackson told him ice tea would be great.

"Sorry, I forgot you are a preacher." He told the lady who came in the room to bring them some ice tea.

They started looking over the breeding papers for the livestock. He would love to buy all of them. It would take him years to build his herd up to this. He asked Jasper what he was asking for the entire herd.

Jasper gave him a fair price. Jackson knew he could buy them, but it would pretty much clean out his savings and investments. He just couldn't do it. He needed to have operating expenses until he started making money with them.

"Jasper, I would love to buy them all, but I can't run myself low until I start making money."

"Jackson, I will make a deal with you. If you will pay me half now and the rest at the end of five years, I will sign over my rodeo contracts to you. I will have my men help you transport the livestock to your ranch."

"Jasper you have a deal. With rodeo contracts, I can probably pay the rest in less than five years. I run a Youth Camp at the ranch on weekends and every day in the summer. I am hoping to get some of the youth interested in the rodeo. There are some great riders in the bunch."

"It sounds like something I would like to hear more about. I have always been interested in helping keep the youth off the street and doing something they can someday make a living at."

"I will send you information when I get home. We can always use help with finances and with people putting in their time."

The cook came in and told them dinner was ready and the guest room was ready for Jackson. He thanked her and they went in to eat.

"Jackson, we will take a ride around the ranch in the morning. I need to see how many calves are out there. I hadn't counted them in a while."

When they got back from checking on them, Jackson called the ranch to talk to Cal.

"Cal see about hiring a couple more fulltime ranch hands. Have Tom check them out before you hire them. I also need you and George to check out the fences and be sure they are in good shape. I have bought all of 'The Bar-Nun Ranches' livestock."

After he talked to Cal, he called Barbara and told her he needed her to do something else for him.

"I am going to give you my passwords for my bank. I need you to transfer $250,000 to the Bar-Nun Ranch account.

I will call you at the office in the morning and give you all the information you will need, to take care of it."

"Jackson are you sure this is what you want to do? I will do whatever you want, but you are putting a lot of trust in me and I know you don't like me."

"Barbara, where did you get the idea, I don't like you? I was hurt by what you did, but I never hated you for it. I just haven't been able to understand it. I have never stopped loving you. I will always be honest with you. I trust you to take care of

17

this for me. I will call you at the office in the morning. Good-night."

Barbara just stared at the phone. She couldn't believe Jackson just said he still loved her. Oh! how she hoped it was true. She never forgot him or stopped loving him. She hadn't even dated anyone in the last four years, because they weren't Jackson. She knelt beside her bed and asked the Lord to let them find happiness with each other. She asked Him to help her make Jackson understand what happened. She went to bed feeling more relaxed than she has been since Jackson came to Hidden Valley.

The next morning, Jasper and Jackson went to the stables to saddle a couple of horses and ride out to the pastures. Davis was there to meet them. Jackson greeted him and the two shook hands.

"Jackson, when Jasper gets the livestock sold, I will be looking for a new job."

"Davis, do you have to stay in West Virginia? If you are able to relocate, I need some ranch hands."

"Jasper, I'm sorry. I'm not trying to hire your foreman out from under you, but I would love to have him if you are not going to need him."

"I have already told Davis, when the livestock is sold, he is free to find a different job. I am 70 years old and plan to sell the ranch and retire. I want to enjoy the rest of my life, while I am in good health."

"Jackson, I would love to work for you. This is what I've done all my life. I love doing it. If you want me, I am ready to come when you are ready for me."

"Davis, you are hired right now. When Jasper is ready to let you go, come to Hidden Valley."

Jackson liked the looks of the livestock. They were all well cared for. There were a number of bulls, and cows and each cow had a calf by her side. Davis told him he would have the men drive them to the corral today. They went to the pasture where the horses were. There were several in the pasture. He also had six riding horses in the stables at the ranch plus the three they were riding.

"Davis do you know if any of the other men will be looking for work? Is there any you would recommend?"

"Jackson, they are all going to be looking for jobs. Jasper is only keeping one ranch hand and his cook until he gets the ranch sold. I would like to take my brother with me. He is good with the cattle and a hard worker, but he is young."

"Davis, I would like to talk to him. Have him ride with you when we take the cattle to the ranch. This way I can see how he works with the cattle."

When they got back to the ranch it was lunch time.

"Jasper, I need to make a call to my office. I need your information so I can have Barbara transfer the money."

Jasper gave Jackson the information and went in to check on lunch.

Jackson put in the call to his office. When Barbara answered the phone, his heart jumped. He thought he needed to get control of himself.

"Barb, I have the information you need to transfer the money."

He gave her everything she needed. "How are things going there?"

She said everything was fine. She thought he called her Barb it was what he used to call her.

"Barb, if there is a problem with the bank call me." He gave her his cell phone number.

"I will call them right away and get the money transferred."

"Jasper, Barbara is transferring the money right now. You need to check with your bank in about an hour to make sure the money is there."

"Jackson, didn't you date a barrel racer by the name of Barbara Anderson? When she dropped out of the Nationals her father showed up here to sell her horse. He sure was a case for a father. The poor girl was so upset. He kept yelling at her and told her she was no use to him anymore and neither was her horse."

"Yes, I did date her, in fact I wanted to marry her, but she left before I could ask her. Actually, she is the one I was just talking to on the phone. She has been helping at the camp. Did you buy the horse?"

"I bought the horse. He is a great horse. He is out there in the stable. He is so gentle you'd never know he's a stallion. He has sired some really great reining horses in the last four years. I still have one of his filly's out in the stable."

"Would you be willing to sell them to me? I will write you a check right now."

"Don't you want to see them first? I will sell you the two of them for three thousand dollars."

"I don't need to see them. I already know Big Red and I'm sure any foal of his will be great." He got out his check book and wrote him a check.

They talked over what they would haul to his ranch tomorrow and when he would come back for the rest.

"Jasper, I will have Davis take the bulls in his trailer and I'll take the horses in mine. We will leave the following day to come back after the rest."

He called Cal. "Cal, we will be loading the cattle and horses to bring tomorrow. How are the fences? I have hired one, maybe two ranch hands, who work for Jasper."

"Jackson, everything is ready here. Drive carefully and we'll see you sometime tomorrow."

The next morning early, they loaded up the cattle trailers. Davis's brother was there helping. Jackson watched him with the cattle and decided he would hire him. He might be young, but he knew what he was doing. They loaded everything and were ready to be on the road an hour later

Chapter Two

W hen they pulled in the ranch, early in the evening, Cal and George were waiting for them.

"Cal, this is Davis and his brother, Chad. They will be coming to work for us. Cal is my brother and partner."

They shook hands. Cal said he was glad to have them there.

They unloaded the cattle in the corral close to the barn for the night. They took the horses to the stable and unloaded them.

Cal was helping Jackson unload the horses. "Jackson, what a beautiful horse and filly you have there."

"The chestnut horse belongs to Barbara. He was her barrel horse when she was on the rodeo circuit."

Cal looked at him for a minute and then said, "Barbara didn't say anything about a horse coming."

"She doesn't know yet. Her father sold him to Jasper when she left the rodeo. She doesn't know I found him."

"Well it will be a surprise. Did Jasper give him back to her? Or did you buy him for her?"

"Let's just say it is her horse. I don't need you analyzing me. I do enough myself."

"Okay big brother, I think it is good of you is all I'm saying."

Jackson wondered what he was doing. He sure was a contradiction to himself. He just wanted to see her happy. Well it was true anyway. He couldn't wait to see her reaction when she sees Big Red in the morning.

Cal had the bunk house ready for Davis and Chad to live in.

"This is where you will be staying. You will take your meals at the house with us for now."

They all went to the house to have dinner. Joyce greeted them and said she was George's wife as well as the cook and housekeeper.

"Thank you for the dinner it was great." They went back to the bunk house to settle in for the night.

The bunk house has a large room at the end for the foreman. It has a fully equipped office with a single bed and full bathroom. The middle of the building is set up for six ranch hands with thin walls between the beds for privacy and two bathrooms on the other side of the room. At the end is a fully equipped kitchen with a large table and bench seating.

"Chad this is a great place. I think we can be happy here. I have a feeling we will like working here for Jackson and Cal. They seem like great people."

Early the next morning they moved the bulls to the pasture fenced for them. They fed them so they would settle in. There was a large pond in the pasture, spring fed, so watering wasn't a problem.

There was a separate pasture fenced for the broncs. They fed them first and then started moving them to the pasture. When they made sure there was water in the pasture, they went to let the other horses in the corral. He brought two of the saddle horses from Jasper's along with Red Man, the filly and the rodeo stock.

Jackson saw Barbara pulling up to the house. He called her over to the corral. When she was almost there Red let out a loud whinny and ran up to the fence. When she saw him, she ran up to him and hugged his neck. The horse looked like he was in a trance.

She turned to Jackson with tears in her eyes. "Where did you find him?"

"The ranch where I went to buy the livestock was the Ranch your father sold him to."

She threw her arms around him and gave him a hug. She tried to pull away. He held her for a few seconds.

"Jackson, I am so glad you own him now. I can see him and if you let me, I can ride him. I know he has a good home here."

"Barb, you can ride him anytime you want. He belongs to you."

"Jackson, I can't afford to buy him from you. I wish I could, but I will be happy just being around him and riding him. Thank you so much."

"I didn't ask you to buy him. He is your horse. See the chestnut filly over there. She is one of his. I am keeping her and you get to keep Red so just accept it, okay."

"Jackson, we need to have a talk first. If you still want to give him to me, then I will accept him. Until then I will be happy just being able to ride him and take care of him."

"Alright then, I have to make one more run to get the rest of the livestock. When I get back, we will have a talk. Hopefully we can put the past behind us and see where the future might take us. I know I want to take it slow this time though. I hope you can understand."

"I do understand and I agree we should get to know each other again slowly. We are both different people than we were. Me more so than you, I imagine. I have your accounting up to date for you. I have also set up a program for you to keep track of your rodeo livestock. I will show you how it works as soon as you give me their papers so I can input them in the system."

"Thank you, do you think you could keep working here in the office, in the mornings? I don't want to take you away from Hank and Anna, but I could use the help."

"I will talk to them and see what they say. I still have the little one to take care of during the day."

Jackson gave her the paper work on the bulls and horses he bought. He told her there were six more horses to bring and some cows with their calves. Four are ranch horses.

"Jackson, I will work on a program to keep all of your ranch stock separate from the rodeo livestock."

"Barb, thank you. I have to leave again in the morning to make the last trip."

The next morning, Jackson and Davis left with the two trucks and trailers to haul the rest of the livestock. Chad stayed behind to help with the livestock they already brought.

When Barbara brought the children down for breakfast, Anna and Hank were in the kitchen.

"Hank and Anna, I would like to talk to you both about something. Jackson would like me to continue working for him in the mornings. It is up to you. I can take Marcus with me and be home in time for the other children to get home from preschool."

"Barbara, I wanted to talk to you about something too. I have a student Nurse who is not going to make it to graduation and needs a job. Her home life is not the greatest. Would it upset you if we were to hire her to take over for you so you can work full time for Jackson? We won't do it if you don't want to."

"Anna, it would be great. I love the children but I love doing what I am doing there. I went to college to get my accounting degree and I would love to be using it and helping with the ranch."

"Good then I will talk to Susanna and let you know when she can come to work for us. In the meantime, you can go ahead and work for Jackson."

Barbara headed over to the ranch to work on the program she was setting up for Jackson. She stopped at the barn to see Big Red. She couldn't believe he was there. She couldn't wait to saddle him and run barrels with him. She missed him so much the last four years. She didn't think she would ever see him again. She couldn't believe they kept him at the Bar-Nun instead of selling him. She couldn't believe Jackson bought him for her. She had no doubt he still loves her, but she also knew she will have her work cut out to convince him to trust her again.

When she went in the office the phone was ringing. When she answered it, Jackson asked how she was doing? She told him about her conversation with Anna and Hank. She would be ready to work full time for him as soon as the new Nanny can start.

"Jackson, in the mean time I will need to find a place to live. I will have to move so the new nanny can have my room."

"Barb, don't worry, we will work something out. Let me have time to think about it. I don't want the move to cause you any problems."

Jackson thought about what Barbara said. He thought about the foreman's apartment, in the bunk house. It has two doors. The one going into the bunk house can be locked and she can use the outside door. It was small, but she was living in two rooms now. She could eat her meals with them at the house.

When they pulled up to the Bar-Nun it was late afternoon.

"Jackson, you boys come in for dinner."

"Jasper, when we are done hauling the livestock, what are your plans for the truck and trailer Davis is using?"

"I plan on selling them as soon as you are done with them."

"Jasper, I would like to buy them. When we start hauling livestock to the rodeo, I will need both trailers and trucks."

Jasper gave him a price and Jackson told him he would call Barbara to transfer the money to his account.

The next morning, they loaded the livestock and headed back to the ranch. He called Barbara.

"Barb, I need you to transfer money for the truck and trailer to Jasper's bank. When you have time look at the room at the end of the bunk house and see what you think about using it for the time being."

Barbara went out and looked at the room. She decided she could make it work until she found an apartment close enough to drive to the ranch every day.

When they arrived at the ranch the next evening, Jackson noticed Barbara in the arena, riding Red. They were running the barrels and really looked good. The horse was as good as he always was. They were still something to watch.

Barbara was just finishing her run when she saw Jackson pull his rig up to the stable. She waved at him and rode Red over to the fence.

"You both looked good out there. It was almost like the first time I saw you ride at the rodeo."

"He is still the best barrel racing horse in the country. It's like we have never been apart. Thank you, Jackson for buying him.

Hank will be out tomorrow to look over the financials with you. The new Nanny will be starting on Monday."

Jackson saw an SUV pull up. Tyler, Zack, Joy and the Price boys got out. The boys came over and asked if they could help unload the horses. Jackson said to unload the four at the back and put them in the stalls. The other two were rodeo stock and go in the pasture with the rest.

Bill and Rhonda came over and he shook Bill's hand and gave Rhonda a hug. He asked them how married life was treating them. They both smiled and told him great he needed to try it.

Rhonda went over to talk to Barbara. "Hey Barb, what a beautiful horse. When did you get him?"

"Hi Rhonda, Jackson bought him when he bought the others. He actually was my horse when I was barrel racing. He is a great horse."

Cal and Davis drove the rig out to the pasture, they had fenced for the cows and their calves. Chad and George came over to take the two broncs to the pasture where the rest were. Jackson introduced them to Bill and Rhonda.

When the boys came out of the stable to join them, Jackson told them, "there will be some new safety rules at the ranch. With the rodeo stock on the ranch there are certain places you won't be able to go and horses you can't go near."

"Jackson would you ride one of the broncs for us, some time? How about one of the bulls too?"

"We'll see about doing something, okay. Are you all ready for tomorrow and Sunday?"

They told him they came out tonight to see if they could help get everything ready.

Joyce sent Joy out to tell them dinner was ready and for everyone to come in and eat. She made plenty for them all.

28

While they were eating the men talked about the livestock and what they were doing. They talked about the changes at the ranch and how they are going to still keep the Youth Ranch growing.

"I hope to teach the older boys about taking care of the rodeo livestock and the difference in the care of them and the other horses and cattle."

The boys said they would love to learn all they can. Tyler told him the more he and Zack learn the better vets they will be.

Barbara said, "Monday, I will be working full time at the ranch doing the books for it and the Youth Ranch. Anna has a new Nanny starting on Monday."

"Barb, did you get a chance to look at the foreman's room. Do, you think it will work for you until I can figure something else out for you?"

"Jackson, it will work until I can find an apartment close enough to drive here every day."

"Barb, you don't have to look for an apartment. There is one above the garage. It just needs some work done to it. It hasn't been used for years. I'll have Don come out and look at it and fix whatever it needs. It is yours as soon as it is ready.?"

"Jackson, I will be happy to rent it. I will not live in it for free. You are not responsible to give me a place to live."

"Okay, we will talk about it when the work is done. In the meantime, you will not be paying rent for the room at the bunk house."

Barbara thought about everything going on with Jackson on her way home. She was having trouble understanding what he was feeling. Did he care for her or was she just another employee to him? They needed to have a talk and soon, so she knows where she stands.

When everyone left, Jackson sat in his office looking over the financial report, Barbara printed off for him. He couldn't keep his mind on the report. He kept thinking back on his conversation with her. He wished he knew what he was doing. He knew she was confused and so was he. They need to talk and then maybe he can figure out what he wants. He knew she could hurt him a lot worse this time. He wondered if he wants to take a chance. He did know he didn't want her leaving the ranch.

The next morning, everyone helping with the Youth Camp arrived. The kids would be there in an hour so they were all working to have everything ready for the next two days.

Jackson saw Don Price show up. "Don, I need you to go with me to look at the apartment over the garage. I want to see what it will need for Barbara to live in it."

When they got up there, Jackson noticed a living room, kitchen with an alcove for a table and chairs, and two bedrooms with a bathroom between them. It was really a nicely laid out apartment. It needed a good cleaning and painting. The carpet in the Living room and bedrooms needed to either be replaced or tile put in them and the kitchen needed a new floor. He thought he would show it to Barbara and let her decide what she wanted.

"Jackson, it could use some ceiling fans for circulation and I could put in a small air conditioning unit outside the garage with a heat pump and run it to the apartment. I will need to check the plumbing and electrical. I should probably run a few more plugs. I will check the electric box. I could get a crew in here in a couple of days. We should be able to have everything done in two weeks."

"Great, get with Barbara and see what she wants done with the floors and the paint colors. Thanks Don, I appreciate your help."

They went back down and Don went over to talk to Barbara. They went back upstairs together.

When all the kids got there, Jackson sat them down and talked to them.

"There are some new rules you will have to follow. You can't go near the pastures where the horses and cattle are. They are not trained and gentle like the ones at the stable. You will learn the differences between the ranch horses and the broncs used for the rodeo. You will also be learning about the bulls in the far pasture and what they are used for."

"We are going to have a good time on the weekends this school year. In the spring, we will have a horse show. You will be learning a lot of different things this year. I have brought in some more horses. You will each be assigned your own horse. You will take care of your horse and its stall. Now let's go over to the stable and pick out your horse."

"Jackson would it be alright if we brought our own horses over each weekend."

"Tyler, it will be fine with me if your dads are okay with trailering them every weekend."

Bill told him it would be fine. Then he would have more horses for the other kids.

The ranch was up and running again for the weekend, until summer gets there. They were having horsemanship classes, cooking classes, flower arranging, landscaping and self-defense classes. They have a full schedule planned. The number of children signed up for the weekends doubled since last year. Jackson was pleased to see so many young kids wanting to do something besides sitting in the house playing on their computers.

When Hank and Anna got there, Hank and Jackson went to the office. Jackson gave him the financial report Barbara prepared for him.

"This looks good Jackson she sure knows what she is doing. I'm glad she is finally going to do what she went to college for. She seems happy. We are going to miss her, but we know she will be happy working here."

"I am glad she took this job. I was having a time getting everything together for you. I'm a rodeo cowboy not an accountant. I had no idea where to start. I happened to remember she took accounting in college. I was glad she was willing to help me out."

"Have the two of you talked yet? If not, you need to and don't let it go too long."

"I know. I told her we would talk about what happened, now I have the livestock moved. I guess I'm still afraid of what she will say. I keep wondering what I could have done to make her run away."

"There is only one way to find out and you need to do it soon. I know you love her and I'm sure she feels the same way."

"Hank, you do know, sometimes love is not enough. There are other things in your life."

"Jackson, isn't it better to find out how things can go instead of always worrying about the future. You will drive her away if you don't get things out in the open soon."

"You're right and I will talk to her as soon as this weekend is over. It would be hard to find time right now with everything going on here."

When they came out of the office, Joyce and Beth, Don's wife, were working on getting lunch. They told the women "hi" and went out to check on what was happening outside.

Jackson saw Barbara in the outside arena working with some of the girls and their horses. She looked his way and smiled and his heart skipped. He thought he was in deep trouble no matter what she told him.

Jackson and Hank stood outside the arena listening to her explain how they set the barrels for the ride.

"You have to set the barrels in a triangle. (She had two ropes she handed two of the girls.) One barrel is set in the center of the arena. Now one of you take the end of the rope and stand at the head barrel, now you go at an angle down the arena to the end of the rope. This rope is 105 feet long. Now you two do the same on the other side at an angle. Now I need two more girls to take this rope and go between these two barrels, this rope is 90 feet long. Now move the barrels until they are this far apart. This is how the barrels have to be set up. Now we will learn the pattern the ride is done in."

"This is a timed event. If you knock over a barrel your time is increased. The one with the fastest clean run wins."

"Miss Barbara, did you ever win any trophies or ribbons when you were in the rodeo?"

"I won a few, yes. I have them boxed away. Maybe sometime I will get them out and show them to you."

When all the activities were over and their horses were taken care of, they all sat around a bon fire to have devotions and sing Christian praise songs. Jackson and Cal both played the guitar. Later they went in their barracks. Barbara went in with the girls and Cal went in with the boys for the night.

The next morning, they all got up and took care of the chores assigned to them and then went to breakfast. After breakfast, they loaded them in the camp van and headed for Church.

When Church was over everyone came out to the camp for lunch and to spend the day together. The kids showed their parents what they were doing at camp. After the camp fire Sunday night, the children and their families headed for home until the next weekend.

When the children and their families were gone, the adults sat down and talked about how it went. They were all satisfied with the way the children seemed eager to learn and work together.

"Thank you all for your time. I think these weekends will give us a good idea of what to do with the summer camp and what the kids will be interested in. I want them to have a good time, but I also want them to know what it is like to be responsible."

They told him it was a great camp and they were all grateful to be a part of it.

When everyone left, Jackson was tired, but felt good about everything.

"Thank you, God for giving me the chance to do what I am doing. Please bless the camp and the children who come here. God please work in Barbara's and my life and let me know what Your plan is for us. Help me to be patient and understanding when we have our talk tomorrow. If I was in the wrong then show me what I need to do to make it right. Amen"

When Barbara got back to the estate, she finished packing her things so the new nanny could move in tomorrow. She knew she wouldn't get much sleep. Jackson would be wanting to talk tomorrow about why she left him. She asked God to help her. She wasn't sure if she knew the real reason herself, why she ran away. She could think of a lot of reasons, but none of them made any sense to her let alone to someone else.

The next morning when Barbara got to the ranch she went in the office and saw Jackson sitting at the desk looking over some papers.

"Good morning, should I go put my things away and come back later."

"No, I was just going over the breeding records of some of the bulls I bought."

She sat down on the couch in the office. He came around the desk and sat down next to her.

"Barb, we need to have our talk and get it all out in the open so we can go on with our lives."

"Jackson, will you let me tell you something about my life first. I think it will help you understand a little better."

"Okay, I want to know everything I can about you anyway. If you think it will help then I will listen."

Chapter Three

"Jackson, my mother died giving birth to me. My fathers Sister moved in with him to help raise me. My father blamed me for my mother's death and my aunt hated me because she thought taking care of me kept her from finding someone to marry. My father spent my whole life telling me I was ugly, stupid and not worthy of being loved. He even went as far as calling me a murderer because my mother died. When I went to college it was because he figured if I got an education I could work and support him. He bought Red when he found out I joined the college team and could earn money if I won at barrel racing. He took everything I made to gamble with. You already know the rest."

Jackson, was quiet while she was talking. She was afraid of what he was thinking. Did he agree with her father and now hate her?

He finally reached over and took her in his arms. He didn't say anything he just held her.

"I only told you all this, because I want you to know what was going on in my life."

"Honey, can you tell me now why you left like you did. I promise you I will try to understand."

"The day I left I went to find you before my last ride. I wanted to be sure you would be there. When I saw you, one of the girls who always followed the rodeo was there. It looked like you were kissing her. Everything my father said came back to me. No one could love me and I was an ugly person. So, I ran instead of asking you what happened."

"Honey, I was not kissing her. I was trying to push her away. There has never been anyone but you in my life. You are loved. I'm sorry for the life you lived, but you came out of it a strong, lovely woman."

"I know what I saw wasn't what I thought. Deep down I knew then. I was just so unsure of myself and immature. I couldn't accept the fact I could be loved. I understand if you are afraid to take a chance on me again."

"I'm not worried about how you were raised. I still think we need to take it slow. It has nothing to do with anything you just told me. I just want us to really know each other."

"I'm fine as long as you don't hate me. I know I hurt you when I left. I hurt myself too in so many ways."

"Honey, I never hated you. When you first left, I was afraid something happened to you. As time went by, I realized you left on your own and I was afraid I'd done something to drive you away. I've gone through a lot of feelings about it since, but never did I hate you. You can't truly hate someone you love as much as I have always loved you. Can you understand what I am trying to tell you?"

"Jackson, I never knew what it meant to love someone until I met you. We met at the wrong time in my life. I was too immature and had no faith in myself or in God. I never knew him growing up. The only father I knew hated me. I started learning about God in college and then I met you and you talked about him like he was a friend. I have grown in my faith since then and am willing to wait on God's timing now. I love you more than anything or anyone except God."

Jackson told her he needed to get to work and so did she. He gave her a short sweet kiss and told her he would see her at lunch.

When he left, she was staring at the door. What did the kiss mean, she wondered? They were supposed to be taking it slow.

Jackson wondered why he kissed her? What was he thinking of, other than he'd been wanting to ever since he saw her again! He went to the stable and saddled his horse, then headed out to the pasture to check on the bulls. As he was riding, he and God had a long talk. He told God when they got married, he wanted it to be in God's timing not his.

When Jackson rode to the stable, he noticed the construction truck at the garage. He took care of his horse and went over to see how things were going. Don was there with the men.

"Jackson, I decided to pull a couple more men in on this job so we can get it done sooner. I don't like her living in the bunk house even if she does have her own room. It just isn't right. I will have the apartment done in a couple of days. You need to put a new stove and refrigerator in the kitchen before she moves in."

"I'll take care of it. Have the men go ahead and pull the old ones out before you put in the new floor. I notice the walls are all painted and the vents have been put in for the air conditioning."

"The air will be in this afternoon. The ceiling fans are already installed and running."

He headed to the house to eat lunch before he went to town to see about the appliances. He thought he would have Barbara go with him, to pick them out. After all she would be the one using them.

When he went to the kitchen, he saw Barbara helping Joyce get lunch for everyone. He told them "hi" and went to wash up. When he got back the rest of the men were there. They all sat down to eat and Jackson said grace.

"Barb, Don says you need a new stove and refrigerator for the apartment. I want you to go with me after lunch to pick them out."

When they got to the appliance store, he asked if she was okay with an electric stove.

"I don't want to run a gas line in the garage to the apartment."

"It's okay with me. I don't do much cooking anyway. I have a toaster oven I use most of the time."

When they picked out what they wanted he asked her if she would like to go have coffee and dessert. She said she would love to.

"Barb, while we are out why don't we go to Roanoke and get the furniture for the apartment. We might as well make a day of it now. We can store it in the garage until it can be placed upstairs."

"Jackson, I don't expect you to furnish the apartment for me. I will get what I need a little at a time."

"No, you won't, the apartment will be furnished before you move in. If you are insisting on paying rent, then it will be rented to you furnished."

"You are so stubborn. I didn't realize how stubborn you were before."

"We are going to go get the furniture. Just let me do this for you. I am not the only stubborn one here."

When they got to the furniture store, he told her to pick out whatever she wanted.

"I don't know anything about picking out furniture."

When she tried to buy just the minimum she needed, he insisted she get everything. The furniture was to be delivered the next day.

"We will put it in the garage and the men can move it upstairs when the apartment is ready."

When they got back to the ranch, they went to the apartment to see how much was done. They were shocked to see it was finished. The floors were all down and new fixtures were in the bathroom. The walls and the trim were all painted. It was ready for the appliances. They were coming in the morning and the furniture would be there after noon. She will be able to move in tomorrow night.

She gave Jackson a hug, "Jackson, it is beautiful, thank you." He held her a little longer before he let her go and told her she was welcome. He thought how good it felt to hold her. He wished he didn't have to let her go at all.

Barbara thought to herself she wished she could stay in his arms forever.

When they went in the kitchen Joyce was setting the table for dinner.

"I wasn't sure you would be home for dinner."

"If I'm not going to be home, I will be sure to let you know ahead of time."

When the men came in to eat, he told them he needed a couple of them to help with the appliances and furniture the next day.

When dinner was over Barbara went in the office to finish what she was working on. Jackson came in and sat down on the couch.

"Do you need something?" He just smiled and said no. He just wanted to be near her.

She saved her work and shut the computer down. Then she went over to the couch and sat down beside him. He put his arms around her. They just sat there for a few minutes.

"Barb, how do you feel about your father and aunt now? You are older and have your life going the way you want it?"

"I feel sorry for them. I really don't think my dad loved my mother. Knowing him the way I do. I think he was angry because she died and left him to do everything on his own. I think my aunt used us as an excuse for not doing what she should with her life."

"Do you ever pray for them? Have you thought about trying to find them and see how their lives are going now?"

"Jackson, I do pray for them. I know it is best my father never knows where I am. He has a bad gambling problem and if he knew I have a good job he would be here trying to get money from me. I'm sure he wouldn't stop at trying to get it from me, but you too. As far as my Aunt is concerned, she could care less where I am or what I am doing. She was just glad to get rid of me when I turned 14."

"You know what is best where they are concerned. I don't want you to do anything if it is not best for you."

Jackson told her he would walk her over to the bunk house. "You will be able to move into the apartment tomorrow."

She thanked him again for everything he did for her. He gave her a quick kiss and told her good-night. Then he went back to the house. After he did his devotions and got ready for bed he laid there and thought about everything she told him about her life

41

growing up. He couldn't understand how any father could be so unkind to his only child.

"Lord I need to find out everything I can about her father. I want to make sure he never bothers her again. Lord I hope the man will someday find You in his life. I don't want Barbara upset by him again."

The next morning Jackson went to the office and asked Barbara what her father's name was.

She asked him why he wanted to know. She was afraid he was going to contact him and it was the last thing she wanted to happen.

"Honey, I don't intend to contact him. I just want to know where he is and what he is doing, so I can protect you."

"His name is Arthur Moriston I changed my last name when I turned 18 to my mother's maiden name. I didn't want to have his name."

"Okay, let's get on the computer and see if we can track him down. We need to know what he is doing and where he is right now."

She put in his name and birthdate in the computer. It came up with his last address in Tennessee and a bunch of arrest warrants for him. He fled the state and all the warrants were outstanding. He disappeared three months ago.

"Honey, I don't like how this sounds. I'm afraid he might try to find you, to help him get out of the country. Barb, please don't go anywhere without me."

"It would be just like him. He can't stand me but he would try to use me to get money. I wish I hadn't found out anything. Now I will be looking over my shoulder all the time.

"Well, I'm glad I had the security cameras and lights put around the ranch and the security fencing and gate. We will start locking the gate at night. I will have the boys watch out for any strangers who might come around."

"Maybe I should have rented an apartment in town. I don't want to bring trouble to the ranch. It won't be good if he comes around when the kids are all here."

"No, you shouldn't have rented a place in town. He would find you and I wouldn't be there to protect you."

"Jackson, it is not your place to protect me. I don't want to bring trouble to you."

"Honey, he may not even be looking for you. He is probably too busy trying to stay ahead of the police. Let's put it in God's hands and wait to see what happens. He won't let us down no matter what happens."

Jackson went out to talk to the men and fill them in on Barbara's father. He said he didn't know what he looks like. She hasn't seen him in years.

"Just don't answer any question if someone comes looking for her. Make sure the security cameras are working and we will close the gate at night."

They saw the delivery truck pull through the gate. It was the appliances for the apartment. The men went to help unload them and Cal said he would hook them up.

With everything he found out this morning, Jackson wished she was going to be living in the house. He called the alarm company and asked them to send someone out to install an alarm in the apartment.

"We have someone working in the area and will get it done this afternoon."

He thanked them and went to tell Barbara about the alarm.

"Jackson, you are doing a lot and he might not even know where I am. I called Hank and told him about my father. If he is looking for me, he will be looking there not here."

"You are probably right. I'm glad you told them just in case."

The furniture arrived right after lunch along with the man from the alarm company. The men helped unload the furniture and took it up to the apartment. Barbara came out to tell them where she wanted it. When they were done, they left and Jackson and Barbara sat down to talk.

They decided they weren't going to worry about her father. She hasn't seen or heard from him in almost five years so he probably didn't know where she was or what she was doing.

"Barb, please be sure to set the alarm when you leave the apartment and when you get home. I will feel better about you living here alone."

"I will try to remember. Thank you for doing all this for me. I wish you would let me pay the rent this apartment is worth."

"I wish you would let me give you the apartment as part of your salary but seeing you won't then you will just have to accept what I charge you."

Barbara went back to catch up on her work. Jackson decided to take a ride out to check on the bulls. While he was riding, he thought about everything happening in his life. He wondered why he was having such a hard time deciding about marrying Barbara. He knew she was the only women he ever wanted in his life.

"God, show me the way. What do you want for us? I do love her more than life itself. Why can't I let go of the hurt from the past. I understand now why she left. Shouldn't it be enough? Lord help me. Amen"

While riding back to the house he felt more at peace after his talk with the Lord. He would wait for an answer and in the meanwhile, they will get to know each other again.

Barbara thought back to when she and Jackson first met and the time they spent together. She realized they really hadn't gotten to know each other. They were so tied up with the rodeo. They went to dinner a few times, but most of the time they were at the rodeo. She looked forward to really getting to know him as the man he is now.

When Jackson got back to the house, he went in to clean-up for dinner. Then he went in the office to see Barbara. He liked having her work there. He could see her whenever he wanted.

"When are you going to show me the programs you set up for the Ranch? I am anxious to see what you have."

"As soon as I know they are working like I want them too. You will just have to be a little patient, if possible."

"Oh, I can be very patient when I have to be. It's when something is important to me, I can get a little inpatient."

"Dinner is about ready and you have worked long enough. I'm going to owe you overtime if you keep this up."

"You don't owe me overtime. I was not working most of the day. We were running around getting my apartment ready, remember."

When he left the office, she thought about what a kind and generous man he was and how different in so many ways to the rodeo star she had known. They really didn't know each other like they wanted to.

Jackson thought to himself, what a different woman she was from the unsure 18-year-old he fell in love with 6 years ago. She was just as beautiful, maybe more so in a more adult way. She was surer of herself and gave back as good as she received, when he teased her. He was going to enjoy getting to know this new person.

When Jackson left the office, he ran into Cal. Cal told him he wanted to talk to him about something.

"What's up little brother? You look like you have something on your mind. Is there something I can help you with?"

"What would you think about me building a house on the ranch? I want to ask Gloria to marry me, but I don't want to live in this house when and if she says yes."

"Hey this is great news. Where would you like to put the house? You can have any place you want and I will deed you five acres."

"Let's take a ride out to the land I am thinking about after dinner. We will still have a couple of hours of daylight."

"Sound like a good idea to me. We will go right after we eat. I'm sure she will say yes. Are you planning on having the house ready before you ask her?"

"No, I'm going to asked her this weekend while she is helping with the Youth Camp. She has this weekend off. I want her to help decide on a plan for the house."

"I think this is great Cal. I have known how you two felt about each other for a while now. She is a great person and I know you will be happy."

"When are you going to jump in big brother? I know you two love each other. What is the hold up?"

"We have to figure it out. Right now, we are just getting to know each other as the people we are now."

"Well it is probably a good idea. Let's go eat so we can take a ride."

"Barbara would you like to take a ride with me and Jackson? I need a woman's opinion on something."

She looked at Jackson and he told her they would love for her to come along.

The three of them went to the stable and saddled their horses. Cal took them out to the far pasture along the back of the property, next to the county road. There are a lot of trees and a small stream running through it. Barbara told them it was so beautiful back there. She hadn't ridden out there before.

"Do you think this would be a good spot to build a house? It is close to the road so it wouldn't be a hard to drive to town and it would be easy to put in a driveway and electric."

"Cal, I think it would be a beautiful spot for a home. Are you and Gloria getting married. I know you two love each other. I have been wondering what you were waiting for. She will love it here."

"What do you think big brother? I would be closer to the bull pasture and I can keep an eye on them from here. These five acres wouldn't affect the rest of the ranch either."

"I think it is a great spot for you. I will have Tom get the deed ready. Bring Gloria out to look at it this weekend. You can start building whenever the two of you decide on what you want. If I were building here, I would build a log house. It would blend in with the woods."

"I love the idea, but it will be up to Gloria. It will be her home too. Thanks brother, I know you won't let me pay for the land, but you should you know."

"Your right I won't. We are partners in the ranch. This is yours no matter what. The deed will be ready whenever you are."

On the way back, Cal thought how lucky he was to be adopted into the family he was. He couldn't have asked for better parents and siblings, even if he got to hand pick them. The Lord sure was good.

"Jackson, I have been thinking about something. I have always wondered about the fact you and Jeff look so much alike and act so much alike. It's almost as if you were twins or blood brothers. Have you ever thought about the two of you having a DNA test done? I know the parents adopted you four years apart and your birthdays are a year apart. It's just something I have thought more about since we are all older."

"We have both thought about how much we are alike, but I don't think either of us have thought about the possibility we are actually blood brothers. You know I think I will talk to Jeff about it."

The more Jackson thought about it on the ride to the house, the more he thought he would talk to Jeff and see what he thought. They both have wondered about the fact the older they got the more they looked alike.

Barbara thought maybe Cal was on to something. She has noticed more than once how much they look and act alike. Sometimes it was like they are reading each other's minds.

When they got back to the stable, they took care of their horses and Jackson walked Barbara to her apartment.

"Barb, don't forget to set the alarm when you go in and lock the door."

"Okay, I will see you in the morning."

He gave her a light kiss and told her good-night.

When she went in, she did what he told her and went to do her devotions before she got ready for bed. She thanked God for the day and for a good man like Jackson to care about her. She went to bed thinking about him and had a good night's sleep.

Jackson kept thinking about what Cal said and decided to call Jeff and see what he thought about them doing a DNA test just to find out.

The next morning, he called Jeff and asked him if he could meet him for lunch. Jeff told him sure, he would see him at the restaurant at noon.

Jackson drove to town and went to the restaurant to meet Jeff. When he came in, they shook hands and Jeff told him it was good to see him. They didn't get to do this anymore with them both being so busy.

"Jeff, Cal brought something up yesterday that I wanted to talk to you about. We have both wondered why we look so much alike and actually act a lot alike. He thought we should have a DNA test to see if we might actually be blood brothers. What do you think about it?"

"To be honest with you, I have the same thoughts from time to time. I can't see it would hurt anything to find out. We can have Beth do the test right there in her lab. Do you want me to call her and see if she has time today?"

"No time like the present to get it done. Give her a call and we can get it done while I am in town."

Jeff called Beth and she told them to come on over.

"It will only take a second and I will have an answer to the question in 24 hours. I remembered our parents talking about Jeff's mother. They knew her and when she got sick, she asked them to adopt Jeff, when she died. They all talked to an attorney and set it up. I have a feeling it won't be a surprise to any of us."

Chapter Four

The next day Beth went to the hospital to talk to Anna and Hank. When she walked in Anna's office, Hank was there with her. "I'm so glad to catch you two together. I need a favor. Jackson and Jeff had me do a DNA test yesterday and I have the results. I want to get all of the family and close friends together to give them the results. I told them it would take longer to get it. I don't want them to know what this is about. Do you think you can help me? I can't tell you what the results are until we are all together, but I'm sure you can make a pretty good guess."

"I will call them and invite them to a BBQ at the estate tonight. I'll just tell them it has been too long since we have all got together for some fun."

"Thank you so much for doing this. You are really great friends. See you all tonight."

"Anna, I will go to my office and get things rolling for the BBQ. How much do you want to bet those two are actually birth brothers?"

"I have thought so ever since Jackson moved here and we got to know them."

At 6:00 that evening, everyone showed up for the BBQ. They were happy to be together. They didn't seem to get the chance anymore.

While they were all sitting down eating, Beth said she has something to tell the family.

"I've something here for Jeff and Jackson"

Jackson looked at her a minute and then realized what she just handed him. He looked at Jeff and then opened it. They read it and then looked over at Beth. She smiled and told everyone. "It looks like our brothers are truly brothers, by blood."

"Guys, I have done some checking and I have a story to tell you both. Let's go into Hank's office and talk."

"When I looked at the results of the test, I decided to go through the boxes of paper work I have of our parents. I planned on doing it, someday but haven't had the time. I found your original birth certificates in the box. It gave your parent's names. Then I found our adopted mother's diary, it told what happened and why you were put up for adoption. Jackson, when you were 6 months old your mother was pregnant with Jeff. Your father was in the army and was killed. Shortly after he died, she found out she had a severe heart problem. The doctor put her on bed rest for the rest of her pregnancy. She had no family living. Her doctor was also our mother's doctor and he asked her if she would be a foster mother for you. After your mother had Jeff, she still wasn't able to take care of both of you so an open adoption was done. She visited when she was able. 6 months later I was adopted, four years later the doctors told your birth mother she was dying. She approached our parents and asked them to adopt Jeff when she died. She asked them not to tell you. She was afraid you wouldn't understand why she gave one of you away and tried to raise the other one. Mom and Dad honored her wish."

"Thanks Sis, I'm glad Mom kept a diary. It helps to know why we were adopted. I wish I could remember her visits, but I can't. I would like to have my original birth certificate and I'm sure Jeff would too."

"Yes, thanks Sis I would like mine too. I would also like to see Mom's diary."

"I'm sure everyone would like to see it. It tells about all our adoptions and information about our birth parents."

When they went back out with the rest of their family and friends, everyone told them they knew they were birth brothers. They were just too much alike not to be.

Cal came over and asked Jackson what Beth told them. "Cal, the five of us need to get together to talk. We will all get together this week."

Jackson told all of his siblings to come out to the ranch on Friday night.

"Beth bring our Mother's diary and anything else you think we should all see."

She told him she would try to look through everything and see if there was anything else.

On the way home Jackson told Barbara what Beth told them. She said she was glad they knew they were loved by their birth mother.

"Sweetheart, I am sure if your mother lived, she would have loved you and protected you."

"I know you are probably right. I just wish sometimes I knew more about her."

"You have the computer in the office. Try to find out about her. There are programs to help you. You know how to do it. When Jackson got to his room, he did his devotions and thanked God for everything they had found out this evening. He always felt Jeff and he had a special bond. He loves all his siblings though. He went to sleep thinking about how much his birth mother must have loved them. He wondered about what kind of man his dad was. He knew he was a soldier.

Barbara went in to do her devotions. She thought about what Jackson said about her mother. She decided to get on the internet tomorrow and see what she could find out about her.

Barbara went in the house early the next morning. Joyce was in the kitchen fixing breakfast.

"Joyce, I will be in the office. I have some things to look up on the computer."

She put her mother's name and birthdate in the computer. It brought up a picture of her and where she was born. It didn't have the date of her death. She decided to go to another site and put in her mother's name and see what would come up. It took her to a Susanna Mae Anderson who in 1989 was named the Jr National Champion Barrel Racer. She was 16 at the time.

Her mother was a barrel racer. Barbara couldn't believe it. Now she knew how her dad knew so much about what horse to buy for her, and she could make money doing it. It was probably also why he hated her so much. Her mother would have quit barrel racing to have her. The money would have stopped when she died. It probably explains why he got so angry when she left the rodeo like she did.

Jackson came in the office to tell Barbara breakfast was ready. He saw her staring at the computer.

"Barb is everything okay. You look like you've seen a ghost. What are you looking at?"

She moved back and let him read what she found. He read it and looked at her.

"Your mother was a champion barrel racer? Have you gone on the Rodeo site to check it out?"

"No, I just found this. I had no idea. My father never mentioned anything about her. It was like she never existed to him."

"Come eat breakfast and then you can go on the rodeo site. They have a place where you can look up ex-rodeo champions and what years they won the titles."

When Barbara went back to the office, she started on the work she needed to do for the ranch. Her search for her mother would have to wait. She was getting paid to take care of ranch business not personal things.

When Jackson came in, he asked her if she found anything on the rodeo web site.

"I haven't gotten on it yet. I will after work."

"Barb it is okay for you to do it now."

"Jackson, you pay me to keep the books for the ranch, not to sit on the computer doing personal things."

"Barb, there is nothing pressing now. You need to find out everything you can about your mother. Please just go ahead and look up the rodeo web site."

Barbara decided to go on the site as long as it was alright with Jackson. When she got on the site, she went to the rodeo Championship winners from 1989 to the present. She put in her mother's name and it came up with 4 Championships from 1989 to 1993, the year she was born. It also had a write up about her. It told about her death in 1993 and how much she was going to be missed on the rodeo scene. It told of her marriage to a bull rider by the name of Arthur J. Moriston when she was 18 and the birth of a daughter in 1993.

"My father was a bull rider? There is no further mention of him on the web site. He must have stopped riding and lived off of what she won. I never knew my father ever having a steady job. He took everything I won to live on and to gamble with. I figured he did the same with my mother."

"I don't remember your father's name being mentioned by any of the older bull riders while I was on the circuit."

"My father was around 10 or 12 years older than my mother. That would make him about 55 or 56 years old now."

"The last time I saw him he looked a lot older than his age. His hair had really started to grey a lot. He was tall but very thin. He was probably 6'2. When I was little, I was afraid of him. He was such a big man with a bad temper. No matter what I did he got angry at me. At one time, he worked on a ranch. It was where I learned to ride. The owner liked me and taught me. It is the only time I remember being happy."

Joyce knocked on the door and told them lunch was ready. Barbara set the printer to print off the information she found and they went to lunch.

After lunch, Barbara went back in the office to see if she could find her mother's death certificate. She thought they lived in Tennessee at the time, but she wasn't sure. She decided to look for her birth certificate at the same time. Her father had her original and she wasn't going to ask him for it.

When she went to the Tennessee department of vital statistics, she found her mother's death certificate and her birth certificate. She ordered them both. When she read her mother's, it stated she died from a severe hemorrhage and complications of child birth. Her birth certificate was signed by a Mid-wife not a doctor. She was born at home instead of a hospital. She might have been alive today if she was in the hospital. It also showed she died the day after Barbara was born. She wondered why her father hadn't taken her to the hospital when she was hemorrhaging. Knowing her father, she figured he didn't want to pay a hospital bill.

She sat there and cried for the mother she never got the chance to know.

When Jackson came in the office, he saw her sitting at the computer crying.

"Barb, what is wrong?" She showed him everything she found about her mother and her death certificate. He read them and took her in his arms and just held her. When she was done crying, he told her to turn it all over to God.

"You don't have to like your father, but you do have to forgive him. I know how hard it is right now, but pray about it, and pray for him."

"I will try, I know it's what God expects of me."

"What do you say, we go for a ride before dinner. You have been at the computer long enough."

They went out and saddled their horses and rode out to where Cal wanted to build his house.

"I am happy for my little brother and I won't be surprised if Meredith and Brad don't decide to get married before too long."

"It looks like the valley is playing match maker again. When people come here, they may as well decide they are going to fall in love."

"Barbara sometime when you need something to do, there is a map of the farm somewhere in the office. See if you can find it for me. I have 1000 acres here and It needs to be utilized. The last owner told me there is still some cattle roaming around, he couldn't find them when he sold the others. I need to try to figure out where they might be hiding."

"I found an aerial map of the ranch in the filing cabinet. I was going to ask you about having it framed and put on the office wall. I think it will help you see where they might be."

"I want to look it over when we get back to the ranch. I need to decide what fields to raise hay and grain on for the livestock. There is no need to be buying it with half of my land just sitting there. We need to head back to the house. Joyce will have dinner ready and be wondering again if we will be there."

When they got back to the ranch house, they took care of their horses and then went to get ready for dinner.

When Jackson went in the house, Joyce told him dinner would be ready in five minutes. He thanked her and went to clean up.

"Cal, Barb found an aerial map of the property. I want to look it over after dinner and see if we can figure out where the stray cattle are. We also need to decide what fields we want to plant for feed. There is already a hay field. It will need to be baled in the spring. We need to get the equipment in the barn checked out to be sure it will be ready."

"I think I can handle it. I did my share of maintenance in the service."

Davis said, "Chad and I did the haying at the Bar-Nun and would be willing to take care of it here."

Chad said he liked working with the machinery and knew quite a lot about it.

"Guys this is great. I was afraid I would have to hire someone. We do need to think about hiring more help though. When the rodeos start in the spring, Davis, George and I will be gone more than we will be here."

"Jackson, there are a couple more good hands at the Bar-Nun looking for work. I can have them get in touch with you if you want."

"Have them get in touch with Cal. He will be the one doing the hiring. I will need to hire at least three more ranch hands and a cook for the bunk house. Joyce does a wonderful job, but I think we need someone for the ranch hands."

"I can come up with three good ranch hands, but I don't think Jasper is ready to get rid of his cook yet. You may need to advertise for one."

"Have the men come here and talk to you and Cal. We will advertise for a cook. I will have Barb put the ad in tomorrow."

"Cal and Barbara, can I talk to the two of you in the office for a minute. I want to look over the aerial map of the ranch and discuss some things with you."

The three of them went to the office to talk.

"Barb, put an ad in the ranch magazine for a ranch cook. Also get some employment papers ready for the men we hire. Have Tom do a back-ground check on them when they fill out the papers." "Cal what do you think about making Davis foreman over the men we are hiring? He would answer to you but the men would answer to him. He was their foreman at the Bar-Nun. George is separate from the other men. He will be working with me at the rodeos. Davis will help haul the stock to the rodeo but will return to the ranch."

"I think it will probably work out great, as I will be busy with the Youth Camp when you are gone. I will have him move in the foreman's room in the bunk house. He will have a computer and Barbara can put whatever he needs on it to do his work."

"Good I will let you take care of interviewing the men. Beth and the rest of our siblings will be here in a little while to show us what she has of Mom's."

Barbara said, "Jackson, I will get out of here so you can all talk. I will place the ad in the morning and put together the employment packages for the new ranch hands."

"Cal, I'll be back in a minute. Barb, I will walk you to the apartment. I need to talk to you a minute."

While they were walking Jackson asked her if she would consider entering the barrel racing at the rodeo again. He would like for her to go with them and participate again.

"Jackson, I can't. My father would find me if I did. It would be the first place he would look for me. Besides, what about the Youth Camp? I love working with the kids. I wouldn't want to give it up."

"Honey, by spring I am sure they will have caught him and he will be in jail. We will figure something out for the kids. It would be good if they could go to a rodeo and see you ride."

"Let's talk about it when it happens. I appreciate the fact you think I could do it again."

"Okay we will talk about it again when it is closer to time for the rodeos to get in full swing."

Jackson saw his family pull up as he walked back to the house. He was anxious to see his mother's diary. They all went in the den to talk. Joyce brought them coffee and dessert. She told them good-night.

Jackson thanked her and told her they could take care of cleaning up later.

Beth made each of them copies of the diary related to their adoption.

"Everyone of us started as foster children. We were all open adoptions with our biological parents having the right to see us and receive pictures and information about us as we grew up. The adoptions were handled through our mother's doctor and their lawyer. Except for Meredith our birthmothers were all sick and unable to take care of us. They all passed away since the adoptions." She gave them pictures of each of their mothers.

Meredith already knew who her mother was and met her. She had no desire to get to know her any better.

They all agreed they were raised by the best parents anyone could have. It was time to count their blessings and thank God for them.

Cal said, "I am going to ask Gloria to marry me this weekend. Please pray she will say yes."

They told him they didn't think he has anything to worry about.

Meredith gave him a hug. "I have news for you too. Brad asked me to marry him and I said yes. We are planning a spring wedding."

They congratulated them and told them how happy they were for them. Jackson said he couldn't have picked out better partners for either of them.

"I am building a house on the county road at the back of the ranch. Jackson is giving us five acres back there."

Jackson said, "Cal, I changed my mind, I've put your name on the ranch with me. You are half owner."

"Jackson, why would you? I don't have anything in the ranch."

"Oh yes you do brother. You have been with me every step of the way since I bought it. You have worked just as hard as I have to build it and the Youth Camp. It is already done. I signed the papers already."

"I don't know what to say. God sure gave me the best family a man could ever want."

They got together in a circle and praised God for what he did in their lives. Jackson said a prayer for their upcoming marriages and asked Him to bless them and keep them in his loving arms.

When everyone left, Jackson told Cal they would go to the bank on Monday and put his name on the ranch account.

"Jackson if I am a partner in the ranch, I want to add my money to yours for whatever is needed for the ranch."

"Cal, fine after you get your house built, but wait until then."

"Gloria will be here in the morning to help set up for the weekend. I intend to ask her then. What if she says no? I don't know what I will do if she does. I have faced some ruthless enemies while I was in the marines, but I was never as scared as I am right now."

"Cal if she says no, you will find out why and then do whatever you have to do to get her to change her mind. I know she loves you. I can see it every time you are together. Just trust God for it to be his timing."

The next morning, Jackson saw Gloria pull up to the house. Cal came out to meet her. He gave her a long kiss and they went in the house. He asked God to have favor on them.

When they came out of the house, they were both smiling from ear to ear. He said, "God, thank you for giving my brother a good help mate."

When they got over to where he was standing, he gave Gloria a hug and welcomed her into the family. She said she couldn't think of a better family to be part of.

Barbara came over and Gloria showed her the ring that Cal gave her. Barbara gave her a hug and congratulated her. "If you need help with anything please let me know."

"We are going to take a ride out to the property where we are building our house. Would you both like to take a ride with us?"

"We sure would. There is time before the kids start coming."

When they got there, Gloria said she loved it.

"Cal can we build a log house. It would look so perfect out here and I have always loved them."

Jackson smiled and said, "Cal what did I tell you?"

"Don't get smart brother. I told you I liked the idea. I just want to be sure it is what Gloria wants."

Barbara said, "I can't wait to see it, when it is built. I love the way it will look in the woods."

Cal said, "We are going to talk to Brad on Monday and see how soon it can be built. We want it done before we get married. We know we are pushing it with winter coming. Maybe we will have a mild winter.

Jackson said, "When it is finished, I will have Ellen and Kurt landscape it for you as a wedding gift. Then if you decide to have the ceremony here it will be ready."

"Jackson, you have done so much for me already. I don't want you to do more."

"Cal, it is what I want to do, please don't take the pleasure from me."

"Cal, you might as well give up. Haven't you learned in all these years how stubborn you brother is?"

"I will have to agree with you. He thinks he is my father instead of my bother. But now I think about it, he has been a second father to me since I came to live with them."

"You better believe it brother and don't ever forget it. Now we need to get back to the ranch or the kids will be sending out a search team for us."

When they got back to the house, Ellen asked Jackson to come over to the front of the house with her and the kids who were interested in landscaping. When he got there. She asked him what he thought about them drawing plans for his front yard and landscaping it. He told her he thought it was a great idea, to go for it.

When he went back to the arena, he saw Barbara in the arena working with the Barrel racing class. Then he went to the inside arena to talk to the boys who were interested in cutting and reining classes.

"First you have to work with your horses and get to know them and let them get to know you. You have to teach them to take their leads at your command. You need them to back at least 30 feet without trying to turn around. Everything is done at a slow canter or lope. When you have your horses working as you want, we will work on the patterns used in the reining and cow horse classes. We will work with each of you and show you how to train your horse."

He told the boys to canter their horses around the arena one direction and change and go the other direction. They watched the horses to see which ones changed their lead automatically. This way they knew which ones would need the most help.

Tyler and Zack had already shown their horses in the reining classes so they rode around with some of the others to help them.

Jackson was watching the horses he bought from the Bar-Nun ranch and knew he got a great bunch of horses.

After the campfire and devotions everyone helping with the camp went in the house to talk about the day. They were all satisfied with what had been done.

Chapter Five

Sunday morning everyone went to Church. After Church, they all went out to the Youth Camp for a cookout and to let the parents see what they were doing at weekend camps. Jackson asked them what they thought about the children coming out on Friday evening, instead of Saturday so they would have more time at the camp.

The parents and the children were all in agreement. Jackson, said to bring them out at 4:00 on Friday nights. The kids were happy. They wanted to spend more time there.

After the campfire and sing along the families left. Jackson, Barbara, Cal and Gloria went in the den to talk about what was happening on the ranch and with the Youth Camp. They were all pleased with what was happening on the weekends with the kids.

"When the kids get here on Friday evening, we can handle everything. The volunteers can still come on Saturday morning for the camp. Friday night I plan to have classes on what they need to accomplish. We will work on what they need to know to get their horses ready for the classes they want to enter in the horse show. We have enough people on the ranch to handle Friday night."

"Jackson, I can put together anything you need for the classes on the computer. I was planning to put diagrams on the computer to show the barrel racers the different patterns for running the barrels. I could do the same thing for you to show the reining patterns for the different classes the boys are interested in."

"Barbara, that would be great. I have diagrams of the pattern for the reining horse and two for the reining cow horse class. The patterns and the rules are different for the two classes. I will get with you tomorrow and give them to you."

Gloria said, "I love working here on the weekends when I am off. Cal, I am on the night shift this week. We can go talk to Brad and Don tomorrow if you want."

"Sweetheart, I will call and make an appointment with them." Then he said to Jackson, "I am going to drive Gloria home. I will see you in the morning."

Barbara said, "Jackson, I am so happy for Cal. They both seem to be very happy and you can tell how much they love each other. They will have a blessed marriage."

"What do you think about us. Will we have a happy marriage someday too?"

"If and when we decide to get married, yes we will have a very happy one. God will be in it and it will be what he wants for us. When the time comes, He will be a part of it and will make it a very good and happy marriage."

While Jackson was doing his devotions, he kept thinking about what Barbara said. He asked God to let him know when the time was right, because he wanted a good and happy marriage with her.

The next morning when he went down for breakfast, he saw Barbara and Joyce working together getting breakfast for everyone. He needed to get a cook for the bunk house because Joyce has enough to do keeping things going in the house for him, Cal, George and Barbara.

"Good morning everyone. Barbara, have you put the ad in the paper and in the rancher's journal for a cook for the bunk house? We have three more ranch hands coming to talk to Cal and Davis about a job.

"I put it in yesterday. If you give me the information you want put on the computer for training, I will get right on it this morning."

"I have some diagrams and information for the reining classes."

When Davis came in for breakfast, he told Jackson and Cal that the new men would be there this morning. They got into town last night.

Cal told him it was great. "When they get here bring them to the office here at the house."

"Davis, I want you in on the interview with me. Barbara has employment papers for them to sign. Have you moved into the foreman quarters at the bunk house yet? If not, you need to do it today."

"Cal, I moved in yesterday and thank you for having faith in me. I think you will be happy with the guys coming for the interview. They are good workers and know the rodeo livestock and their needs."

"Cal and Davis the only thing I want to know is how they will be around the youth when they are here. If they would be willing to help with them when the time comes to teach them about the rodeo livestock."

"Jackson, it will be one of the first questions we will ask them. We know how important it is for anyone working here."

The men went out to take care of the livestock and Jackson and Barbara went into the office to work on the computer program for the Youth Camp.

"Jackson, show me what you want put in the presentation for the training sessions."

He showed her the diagrams and information he wanted in the presentation. "I can scan it to the computer and put it in a presentation for you."

Jackson heard trucks coming up the lane. When he looked out the window, he saw three pickups pulling horse trailers pull up to the stable. "Barb, I will be right back."

When he got to the stable, Cal and Davis were coming out to meet them. Davis introduced them to him and Cal. They were the men who came for the interview as ranch hands.

"Why don't you come on in the office when you get your horses in the small paddock. Barbara has the employment papers ready. We will turn the office over to you."

When they went into the office, Davis introduced the men to Barbara.

"Barbara, this is Phil Sanford, Kevin Whitman and John Zanders."

They told her "hi" and it was a pleasure to meet her. She told them "hi" and gave the paper work to Davis and left the room with Jackson.

"They look like a nice bunch of men. I hope they are all Davis says they are. I will call Tom as soon as I have their papers so he can do a background check for you."

"I'm going to have to figure out where to put their horses for now. Both stables are full, I guess we can use the stalls in the small barn for now. They will be needed for the horse show though."

When Cal asked them about the youth, they said they would love working with the young people. Phil told them he attended something like it in Colorado where he came from. He loved it and learned a lot.

Cal felt good about them. "We will be doing a background check on all of you. It is required by the state because of working with the youth."

They told him they were okay with it. They've had them before and it didn't worry them.

"I will take you out to the bunk house and get you settled in."

"What about our horses? It looked like you have a pretty full stable."

"If I know my brother, he already has it figured out."

Cal gave their paper work to Barbara and she called Tom to do the background check. She put their information in the computer so they would be added to the payroll.

"Jackson, what about their horses? I have a good feeling about all of them. They all liked the idea of the Youth Camp and one of them attended something like it in Colorado where he is from."

"Cal, have them use the stalls in the small barn for the time being. We will have to figure something else out before the horse show though. I'm going to talk to Brad and Don about whether we should add onto the stables we already have or build a new one."

Barbara was on the phone when they came in. When she hung up, she told them she had a call from a man about the cook's job.

"I've set up an appointment for him to come in for an interview tomorrow. I got enough information from him to have Tom do his background check."

They thanked her. Cal asked her to call him when the man got there the next day. She told him she would. His name is Dalton Primes.

When Cal went out to talk to the men about their horses, he asked if any of them knew Dalton Primes.

Phil said, "I worked with him on another ranch. He is a good cook and handy to have around if we needed an extra hand."

Cal said, "I like hiring people who know each other. It makes the working situation easier on everyone."

"Jackson one of the new men knows the man coming for the cook's job."

He told him what he said about the man. Jackson said it sounded great.

"Jackson, I have scanned the diagrams you gave me into the computer. I will put them on a presentation for you to show the youth interested in the reining classes. They should be ready for you this weekend. I will put it on my laptop so you can take it in the arena to show them."

"Barb, thank you so much. Maybe I can take a look at them later. I need to go talk to Don and Brad right now about building another stable."

Jackson drove to town to talk to Don and Brad about the new stable. He decided it needed to be a new one. He has different ideas for it than what the others are like.

"Hi Brad, how are you doing. Have you and Meredith set a date for your wedding yet? I haven't had a chance to talk to my sister since you told us about your engagement. Is your Dad around? I need to talk to the two of you about a job I need you to do."

"Hi Jackson, He's gone to lunch, but he should be back soon. I have been working on the Log house for Cal and Gloria. What is it you are needing? I think most of my business anymore is with your family."

Jackson told him he needed to build a new stable, but it was going to be different than the two he has now.

"This one will be a lot wider and longer. I want two large foaling stalls with a wide isle between the stalls. I want an office at one end, a wash area for the horses and twelve other stalls, six on each side. I know the construction will most likely have to wait until spring, but I want to have the plans ready to go when your Dad is ready. Cal and Gloria's house has first priority."

"I would show you the house plans, but I think your brother would like to be the first to see them."

"I'm sure your right. I guess I'll just have to wait, but I bet it will be beautiful."

Don came in while they were talking. Brad filled him in on what Jackson wanted.

I have two crews finishing up their jobs this week. I can do both Cal's house and the stable. I should be able to get the foundations in and possibly get the house covered before bad weather. I might even be able to get the stable up before then."

When he got back to the ranch, he told Cal to come into the office to talk.

"Cal, I am planning to build another stable. It will be larger than the ones we have now. What do you think? You are my partner so you have a say in what we do here. By the way Brad said to tell you the plans for your house are ready for you and

Gloria to look at and approve. He wouldn't show them to me. He said he needed to show you first."

"It's great, will Don be able to handle my house and the new stable? I don't want to wait too long to get the house done. We would like to get married in the spring."

"He told me he has enough crews to get them both done. If he doesn't, he can hold off until spring to do the stable."

"Jackson, I have a feeling you have something more going thru your mind about the ranch. What are you thinking of doing?"

"I thought Jeff was the only one who could read my mind. Yes, I have been thinking about something since I have the rodeo stock. What do you think about running a camp for rodeo riders to come practice and hone their skill? We would still have the Youth Camp and let the kids learn more about rodeo life."

"I tell you what. Let me put away what the house is going to cost, then I will put the rest of my savings with yours and see what we come up with. I think it is a good idea and will bring more revenue for the ranch. We would have to build another bunk house so they could stay here while they are training. I see why you are building another stable and a larger one."

Barbara asked, "Jackson, would it include a barrel racing clinic? I would like to be a part of it if it would."

"You know Barb, I think it's a good idea. We will need two new bunk houses. We will need to have one for the girls."

"I have some money saved. I could build the one for the girls. I think it is really a good idea and I know it will work."

"Barb, I have a rodeo coming up the first of the year. I have a contract to deliver a couple of bulls and three horses. I can ask around while I am there and see what interest I get."

"Jackson, I heard back from Tom and he said the guys were cleared to start. He also checked on the cook who is coming tomorrow for an interview and he looks good too."

Cal went out to check on the men and to make sure the kitchen was ready for someone to cook in. He checked out the stove and refrigerator and they both seemed to be in good working order. He left the refrigerator on so the cook could go buy groceries for the bunk house.

"Jackson, I have been working on the computer to get it ready to use for training the Youth. I am ready to move the diagrams onto the program to see if you like it."

"I'm anxious to see what you've done. I couldn't do all of this without you. I really appreciate what you've done for me. I think I should be paying you a lot more."

"Jackson, you pay me plenty. I don't do it for the money. I love doing things to make the Youth Camp better and I love helping you with it. I hope this will help them while they are learning. At least they will have something to visually look at."

"This will be great. This way they will have something to study. I can tell them what they need to do but being able to see it and study it will make a big difference.

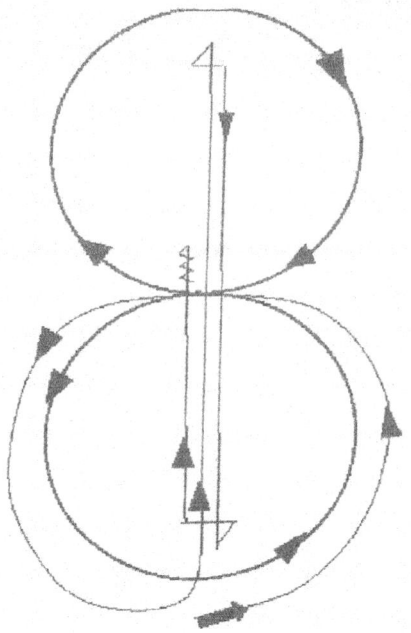

"This first one is for the Reining class pattern."

Here is the information on how to run the course. Please let me know if there are any mistakes. Then I can make copies for the kids to study while they look at the diagram.

1. Enter the gate on the left lead, loping in. Lope one circle left.
2. Change leads (simple or flying)
3. Lope one circle right
4. Change leads (simple or flying.)
5. Continue on the left lead around the end, continue up the middle of the arena past the end maker. Stop
6. Make one and a half spins left.
7. Continue down the middle of the arena, past the end marker. Stop.
8. Make one and a half spins right
9. Continue down the middle of the arena past the center maker, Stop. Back at least 30 feet.

This pattern may be adjusted to suit the arena layout and conditions by the Judge.

Cow Horse reining pattern

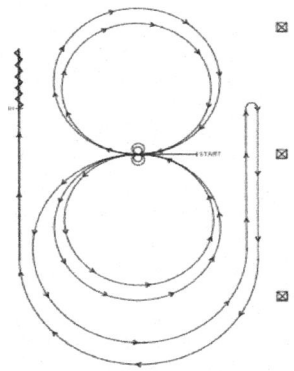

"This pattern is to be used by youth 10 and under. Short stirrup class only."

Horses may walk or trot to the center of the arena. Horses must walk or stop prior to starting the pattern. Beginning at the center of the arena facing the left wall or fence.

1. Beginning on the left lead, complete two circles to the left. Stop at the center of the arena. Hesitate.
2. Complete two spins to the left. Hesitate.
3. Beginning on the right lead, complete two circles to the right. Stop at the center of the arena. Hesitate.
4. Complete two spins to the right. Hesitate.
5. Beginning on the left lead, go around the end of the arena, run down the right side of the arena past the center marker, stop and roll back right.
6. Continue around the end of the arena to run down the left side of the arena past the center marker. Stop. Back up.
   Rider must dismount and drop the reins to the designated Judge.

Cow Horse Reining Pattern 11

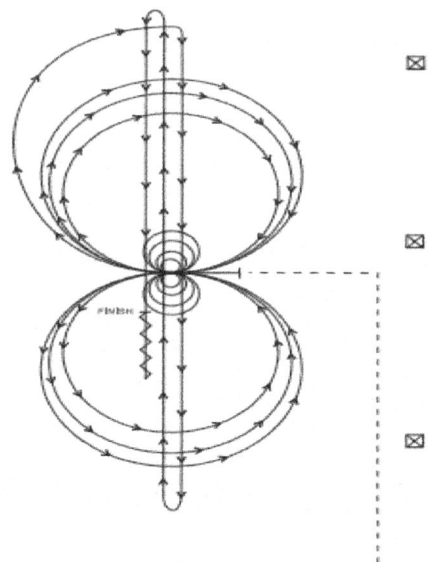

Horses must trot to the center of the arena. Horses must walk or stop prior to starting the pattern. Beginning at the center of the arena facing the left wall or fence.

1. Complete four spins to the left. Hesitate.
2. Complete four spins to the right. Hesitate.
3. Beginning on the right lead complete three circles to the right. The first circle small and slow; the next two circles large and fast. Change leads at the center of the arena.
4. Beginning on the left lead complete three circles to the left. The first circle small and slow; the next two circles large and fast. Change leads at the center of the arena.
5. Begin a large circle to the right but do not close the circle. Run down the center of the arena past the end marker and do a right roll back-no hesitations.
6. Run up the middle of the oposite end of the arena past the end marker and do a left roll back-no hesitation.

7. Run past the center marker and do a sliding stop. Back up to the center of the arena or at least 10 feet. Hesitate to demonstrate completion of the pattern.
    Rider must dismount and drop reins to the designated Judge.

"Have you done one for the barrel racers too?"

"Yes, I have and I think you are right. The diagrams will help them understand what we are talking about better. I think it gives them a whole new Perspective on what they are doing. I am looking forward to using them this weekend and see how they work for them, especially the new girls.

This diagram shows them how the barrels are to be set up.

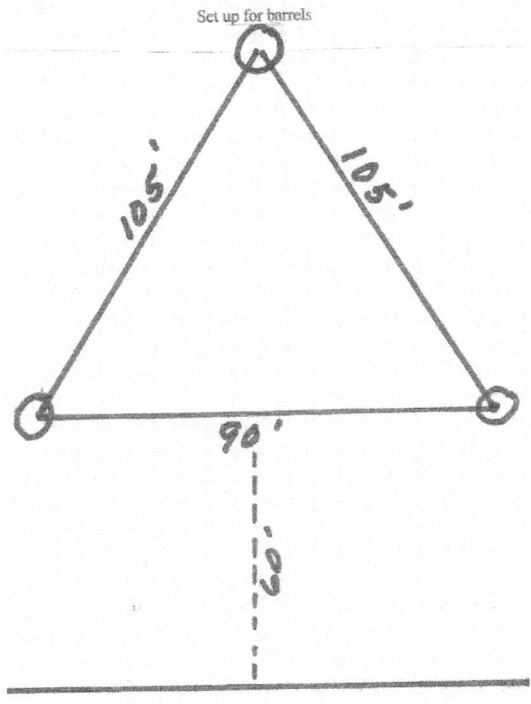

"The diagram below shows the patterns the run is made.

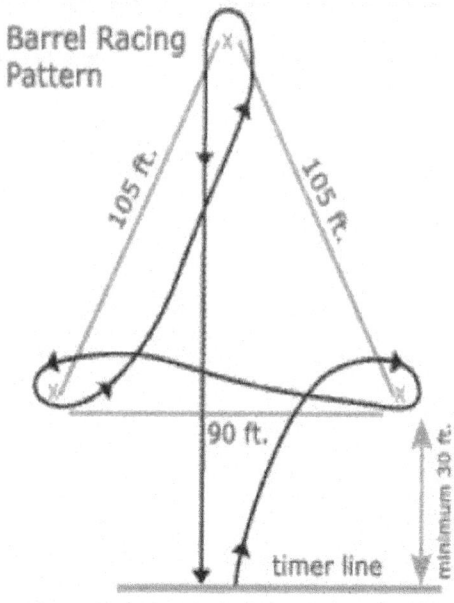

in."

Barrel Racing Patterns

You can start your run from either the right or left. Whatever is most confortable for you and your horse. The timer starts the second you cross the starting line. The clock stops the second you cross the line at the end of your run. You need to control your speed around the barrels. If you knock over the barrel your time is pentalized 5 seconds. If you knock over the barrel you need to complete your run so you don't confuse your horse.

When you round the last barrel it is time to let your horse go. By this time the horse is ready to run full out. Encourage him by giving him full rein. The one with the fastest and cleanest run is the winner.

To run the left pattern reverse the run for the right run.

Chapter Six

The man applying for the cook's job knocked on the door. Barbara went to answer it. When she answered it, she was shocked? She knew the man as Cookie. He was called that at the ranch her Dad worked at for a while when she was 14 years old.

He smiled at her and said, "Can this be, are you little Barbie?"

"Cookie, is it you? How can you remember me after all these years? It has been 10 years since you have seen me."

"We all became very fond of you when you were at the ranch. I never understood your father treating you the way he did. You don't know how many times I wanted to beat him. The only reason the boss kept him on was because of you. We worried about you when he took off with you like he did."

"I loved being on the ranch. I missed all of you so much when we left. I wanted to say good bye but he wouldn't let me."

"I didn't realize it was you applying for the cook's job. I didn't know your real name. You have always been Cookie to me."

Jackson came in the house and saw them talking.

"Barbara, do you know him?"

"I do. Cookie is one of the reasons I liked it so much on the ranch my Dad worked on for a while"

They went in the office to talk. "The job is yours if you want it. I will give you a credit card to buy what groceries you need for the bunk house. When can you start?"

Cookie told him he could start immediately.

When he left the room, Jackson asked Barbara, "I take it he knows your Dad. He wouldn't tell him where you are, would he?"

"He didn't like my Dad. Cookie and the owner kept him away from me as much as they could when I was on the ranch."

"Good to know. I think we need to get in touch with the Tennessee police and find out if they've found him yet."

"Jackson, I think maybe you are right. I was thinking about talking to Mark Williams about my father, just in case he does show up here."

"Honey, I will give Mark a call and have him come out to talk to you and in the meantime, I will call Tennessee and see what I can find out."

Jackson went out to the bunk house to talk to Dalton about Barbara's father.

"We think her father may be looking for her. He has a bunch of warrants out for him and the police haven't been able to find him. I am afraid he is trying to find her in order to get money from her. If you see him around town let me or Cal know."

"I will keep an eye out for him. Her father is no good and I don't want to see him around Barbie either."

Jackson thought to himself, God sent Dalton there for a reason. He was the only one who knew what her father looked like except for Barb.

When Jackson talked to the Tennessee police, they informed him her father had been seen as far as West Virginia. He seemed to always be a step ahead of the local authorities.

"His daughter lives here in Hidden Valley and I'm afraid this is where he is headed."

He gave them Mark's telephone number and asked them to get in touch with him and send him a picture of her father.

They thanked him for the information and would also send an FBI officer there. When he crossed the state line it became an FBI issue.

Jackson went ahead and called Mark and asked him to come out to the ranch and talk to Barbara. He told him he would be out within the hour.

He went into the office to let Barb know Mark was coming out to talk to her.

"Barb, your father was seen in West Virginia. The FBI is looking for him now. When he crossed the state line it became their jurisdiction."

"So, he is looking for me and knows where I am. We need to warn Anna and Hank. I am sure he thinks I work for them."

"I have already called Hank and let him know. He has informed his men to look out for him and told Nanny to keep the children inside until he tells her otherwise. They are keeping their gates lock and I have locked ours. When someone buzzes to come in the security camera will show you who is at the gate and you can buzz them in."

"You mean the men will have to be let in and out? Won't it be hard on them every time they want to go into town for something?"

"No, they all have the code for the gate. They can let themselves in and out."

While they were talking the buzzer went off. When she looked at the screen, she could see it was Mark Williams from the police department. She pushed the button and the gate opened to let him in. She smiled at Jackson.

When Mark came in the office Jackson shook his hand and Barb gave him a hug and asked how he was doing. He showed them the picture of her father the police in Tennessee sent him.

"He is a little grayer than last time I saw him, otherwise it looks just like him."

"I have the department looking for him. If he shows up here, he will be arrested and handed over to the FBI. If you hear from him or see him anywhere let us know. I have given a picture to Hank just in case he thinks you still work there."

"Thank you for coming out. I feel better about everything knowing you are watching for him. I don't fear for my life, but I do know he can be dangerous if he is cornered; so be careful."

"Don't worry, we will handle him if he shows up in Hidden Valley. No one will tell him where you are if he asks around town. What I have found out in the two years I've been here is the valley takes care of her own."

They thanked Mark and told him to come out some weekend when he is off and see what they do at the Youth Camp.

"Mark, I would like you to talk to the youth sometime about law enforcement. Seems these kids have had only bad experiences with the police force and I think it would be good for them to hear from you what the police actually do."

He told Jackson he would love to. He would let him know when he has a weekend off.

Don called Jackson while they were talking.

"Jackson, I was out where Cal is having us build his house. I noticed a dark green pickup sitting along the road with North Carolina plates. There was no one in sight though."

While Jackson was talking to Don, Cookie came in and told Barbara he had seen her father in town. He drove away in a dark green Ford 150 pickup.

When Jackson got off the phone, he called Davis.

"Davis, get some of the men and go out to the bull pasture. If whoever was in the pick-up, whether it is Barbara's father or someone else they will be in trouble if they try to cross the bull pasture. Those bulls will charge anyone on foot."

"Barbara, call Mark and tell him what is going on. We think it's your father. Hopefully we will get to him before the bulls do. I hope he has better sense than to cross a bull pasture."

The men had already headed out to the pasture. Jackson and Cal saddled their horses and headed out to make sure everything was okay. When they got there, they saw Davis ride between a man who was standing in the pasture with a bull about 100 yards away, pawing the ground and snorting. Davis rode between them and pulled the man on to the back of his horse while the other men herded the bull back to where the others were.

When Davis brought him out of the pasture, he ordered them to take him to his daughter.

Jackson rode up and told him he'd best settle down or they might put him back in the pasture.

"Who do you think you are? I want to see my daughter right now."

"In the first place, I happen to be the owner of this ranch and you are trespassing."

"Well, I know my daughter works here and I need to see her."

"What makes you think your daughter works here and if you are sure why did you try to come through the pasture instead of coming to the house?"

"Because I saw you have a security gate, and I didn't want anyone to know I was here. I know she works here because she is the only woman stupid enough to teach kids to barrel race instead of doing it herself."

"Davis, take him to the house, but do not let him go inside. Mark should be there by the time you are."

When they headed for the house Jackson called Barbara and told her, they have her father and are on the way to the house with him.

"Mark is here and I told him to put the police car in back so my father wouldn't see it. The FBI are on the way to pick him up."

When they rode up to the house, Mark came off the porch and arrested her father. He kept saying he wanted to talk to his daughter.

Jackson went in the house and asked Barbara if she wanted to see him. She walked out on the porch with him.

"You have to get me a lawyer. You are my daughter and you have to do this for me. It needs to be a good one."

"I have no intention of doing anything for you. I don't have a father, he died with my mother years ago. I have no desire to do anything for you. You have taken all you are going to from me."

She turned around and walked in the house. When she got inside, she prayed to God and asked him to forgive her. She could feel nothing but pity for the man out there. She asked God to help him find his way. It was all she could do for him.

When the FBI pulled up Mark turned him over to them. He was still hollering for Barbara. She needed to come out, and help him.

Jackson thought to himself he'd never seen such an arrogant man before in his life. He was glad it was over and Barbara could put the past behind her.

He went in the office to make sure she was alright. She was sitting in her chair staring out the window. He went over and took her into his arms and just held her. He didn't know what to say to her so he just held her while she cried for the father she never really had. When she got hold of herself, she thanked Jackson for holding her and caring.

"Barb, I love you, of course I care. I know this has all been hard on you. Sweetheart, it is all over now and you can live your life without worrying about what he is going to do. I fell in love with you the first time I saw you when you were 17 years old. I was 23 and couldn't do anything about it other than to be your friend."

"Well, I had a teenage crush on you then too. I couldn't believe a famous bull rider would want to be my friend. I can't tell you how many times I wished I was older and could date you. When you asked me out on my 18th birthday I couldn't believe it."

"I was afraid you would think I was too old for you and not want to go with me. I can't tell you how relieved I was when you said yes. I knew you were too young and inexperienced then and I understand now why you left. I wish I understood all of this then. We have a second chance to have a good life together and I hope soon you will decide to give it a try. In the meantime, I am happy to get to know you better and wait until you are ready. I love you so much."

"Jackson, the FBI have left to take her father back to Tennessee for trial. They told me he is looking at 15-30 years in the federal prison."

Jackson told Barbara what Mark said. She thanked him and went back to her desk to work on the computer.

"I still have some work to do on the things for the Youth Camp this weekend."

"Barb, turn off your computer and let's go for a ride. You've had enough excitement for the day. We both need to relax a little before dinner."

"I would love to, Jackson. Let me save this and I will quit for today. I can get a fresh start tomorrow. Maybe my head will be a little clearer."

They decided to ride back to where Cal was building the house. Cal went to town to have dinner with Gloria at the hospital, she was working the afternoon shift. They told Joyce not to wait dinner on them. They would get something when they got back.

When they got out to where the house was being built. Jackson remembered Arthur's truck being by the road. He went to see if the keys were in it. They needed to get it off the road so no one would run into it. He saw the keys were in the ignition. He called Davis and asked him to bring someone out there to drive it back to the house.

"Jackson, why are you worried about taking care of his truck?"

"Honey, I am not worried about taking care of it. It is sitting on the county road and I don't want someone running into it at night.

I will call Mark when we get back to the house and ask him what they want to do with it. They will probably impound it until after his trial."

"I'm sorry, I guess you are right. We do need to move it off the road. I just don't want anything to do with anything belonging to him."

86

"Honey, I do understand and I will get it moved off the ranch as soon as I can. Now what do you think of where they are building the house. They have the foundation poured. At the rate, they are going they will have it done by spring. Don said they will probably have it in the dry in a couple of months."

"It looks like it is going to be big. I love the way it will set up against the woods. It is such a beautiful place for a home. I am so happy for them."

"Barb, when we get married would you want to build a new house? We can if you don't want to live in the one, I have.?"

"Jackson no, I love the house. The only thing I think you should think about is taking out the double windows in the office and put in French doors so people can come to the office without going through the house. The porch wraps around there so it would be easy access to it from the porch."

"Honey, it's a great idea. I will talk to Don and see when he can do it. It is inconvenient for people to be coming through the house all the time. I've been thinking about some other changes I want to do at the house. Maybe some time we can look the house over and talk about some ideas I have for it."

"Why do you want me to look it over with you? Whatever you want to do with it is up to you."

"I like your ideas and I hope someday you will be living there too. I do plan on us being married someday. When you are ready and the Lord says it is time. I just want us to take the time to really know each other."

"I want it too. I feel like I know you as you are now and I realize if I'd really known you four years ago, I wouldn't have reacted the way I did. I am sorry for it now, but I think it was God telling us it was too soon."

"We will know when the time is right. For now, I am happy just knowing you are here with me and someday when the time is right, we will be married and it will be with God's blessing."

"Jackson, I did love you back then, but I was too immature to handle what life had in store for me. I am stronger now and my love for you is deeper than it has ever been. I don't mind waiting as long as I am here with you."

"We need to head back to the house. It will start getting dark soon. I hear the guys coming to get the truck off the road."

He waved to the men and they started home. He thought how he wished they could get married right now, but he would be patient and wait for the time to be right.

Barbara was thinking about everything they talked about on her way to the house. She was anxious to see the rest of the house. She'd never been upstairs. The office at one time was the master suite. It is why it has its own bath room and a walk-in-closet full of file cabinets.

When they got back, they went in the kitchen and fixed something to eat. They took their food to the office to eat.

"Barb, I am going to Roanoke in the morning and rent a plane to look for the cattle."

"Jackson, are you going to ask Jeff to fly you. I know he has his pilot license. Didn't he fly supplies to the areas he worked in South America?"

"Yes, he did, but I also have my license. I used to help him fly supplies when he wasn't able to. We both took lessons together and got our license at the same time. Would you like to go with me and be my spotter?"

"I would love to. I didn't know you flew too. Is it alright for me to be away from the office tomorrow? You pay me to work in it."

"The last I knew I was the boss. If I want you with me it is my choice. Besides you will be working. You will be helping me find the cattle. We will leave right after breakfast. I will call and have a plane waiting for us."

The next morning after breakfast they left to go pick up the plane. Barbara had the aerial map with her. They will be able to use it to determine the ranches boundaries and the area where the cattle might be.

When they got in the air, Barbara couldn't believe how beautiful everything was. She'd never been in a small plane before. She was surprised she wasn't afraid. She knew Jackson would keep her safe.

"What do you think? Are you okay flying with me in this small plane?"

"I love it, I was just thinking of how beautiful it is up here and how small everything looks below us. According to the map we are getting close to your land."

"Actually, I think we just crossed over onto it. Check the map with the mountain range. It should mark the south boundary of the property. We need to start looking for any signs of them."

Jackson flew lower and she kept looking for any signs of movement among the mountains and wooded area. They were flying for a while when she saw them.

"Look Jackson, there they are and they have a bunch of calves with them. You have a whole herd down there."

"Well I'll be. There sure is a bunch of them. They look like Black Angus. There are enough to feed the ranch and sell too. Mark the area on the map and we will have a round up next week."

"Let's head back to the airport and we will show the men where they are."

"Jackson, make another pass, I have my camera with me and we will take a picture of them and the area."

"That is a great idea. Thank you for thinking of bringing your camera. A picture of the area will help."

When they got back to the ranch, Jackson asked Cal and Davis to come to the office. He showed them where the cattle are on the map and then they looked at the pictures Barbara put on the computer for them.

"Jackson, we will need more men for the round up. There are more cattle than we thought there would be with all the calves."

"I will talk to Hank, Bill and Tom and see if they have men, they can spare for the round up."

"We need to decide where we are going to pasture them. We will need a large area and it has to be away from the rodeo bulls. We will decide which ones we will sell off. I will have to decide which ones to butcher for their meat and then it will be easier to know how much pasture we will need for them in the future. First, we have to get them rounded up and moved closer to the ranch area. They are good looking Black Angus cattle."

Jackson called the others and asked them and their families over for dinner the next evening. He told them he needed to talk to them about something. They said they would be there.

The next evening after dinner the men went into Jackson's office to talk.

"We found the cattle the previous owner told me were on the land. There is a lot more of them than I thought there would be. We will need to have an old fashion round up to get them to the compound."

They told him they would love to be a part of it and they could each bring along several of their ranch hands to help.

Jackson told them he would find a chuck wagon to take with them and Dalton would come along to cook for them.

"Jackson, have you thought about asking the school if they would let the four older boys out of school for a few days to go on the round up. I think it would be a great experience for them."

"Hank, that is a great idea. I will call the principle in the morning and see if we can get permission to take them. I'll call the Price's tonight and make sure it will be alright with them. Bill will you check with Mark and see if it is alright for Zack to go?"

"I'll check with Mark and I know Tyler and Zack will be thrilled to go. Mark will probably want to go too."

When everyone left, Jackson told Barbara he needed to call the school in the morning and get permission for the four older boys to go on the round up. He also needed to find a chuck wagon for Dalton to use to fix meals for the men.

"Jackson ask Davis about it. I remembered them having one at the Bar-Nun when I was there. Maybe they still have it. You will have to take the open top cattle trailers to get it if they do."

The principle gave his permission for the boys to go. He said he wanted them to take pictures and tell the other students about the adventure when they got back.

"Davis, does Jasper still have the chuck wagon Barbara told me about."

"As far as I know he still does. I'll call him and find out. It would be ideal for the round-up."

When Davis called Jasper, he said he still has it and he wanted to go with them on the round-up."

Davis told him they would send a truck and trailer for him and the wagon.

Jackson, Cal and Davis went to check the fencing in the area for the cattle. There was about 100 acres fenced on the other side of the ranch, away from the rodeo livestock. They rode the fence line to make sure it was ready for the cattle. Now all they had to do was get everyone together to decide on when to go.

They decided they would go on Monday. It would give Chad time to go after Jasper and the chuck wagon. Barbara would call the principle and let him know the boys would be out of school for a few days. And they would have time to get everything ready.

"Jackson, I wish I could go, but I know it's not possible. I need to be here to take care of the ranch business."

"Honey, I need you to check around for buyers for some of the cattle and find out where we can get the meat processed when we bring them in and pick out the ones to butcher."

"Jackson, I don't like having them butchered. They are so beautiful. I know it is part of life, I guess I am a softy."

"Honey, the only reason black angus cattle are raised by ranchers, is for their meat. I'm afraid we can't just keep them for pets."

Jackson called Chad into the office and told him he wanted him to take the larger cattle trailer and his truck and go to the Bar-Nun and pick up Jasper and the chuck wagon. They will leave on the round-up early Monday morning.

"Jackson, I will leave early in the morning. I should be back in a couple of days."

"Jackson, there should be everything I need in the chuck wagon to cook with. All I need is to get the food to cook. The food you take on a round-up is different from what you normally cook. We will be eating a lot of beans and chili and stew on the trip along with eggs, bacon and pancakes."

"Well Cookie it doesn't sound bad to me. Go get whatever you need. Chad will leave in the morning to get Jasper and the chuck wagon."

Chapter Seven

Friday, after lunch Jackson saw Chad coming up the lane. He went out to meet him and Jasper. When Jasper got out of the truck, he told Jackson he loved his ranch.

"You have a beautiful place here, Jackson. I am anxious to meet the Youth you have coming here this weekend. Chad has been telling me about all the things you have planned for them."

"Welcome Jasper, we are happy you could come with Chad. I guess we should go help Chad unload the chuck wagon. Did you have a good trip? Thank you for the use of the chuck wagon and for coming to go on the round up."

"I am looking forward to it. It is good to see my old employees again and to know they are happy working here. I brought you another present with the wagon and I think we better get over there and help unload."

When they got there, Jackson noticed Chad and Davis were unloading two beautiful draft horses from the back of the trailer

"I thought you may need horses to pull the wagon. They are the ones we always used in the parades at home. They are well trained and very gentle."

"Thank you so much Jasper. I don't know what else to say. I was trying to decide which of my horses to use to pull it."

Barbara came out to the barn to see the wagon and horses she saw being unloading. She gave Jasper a hug and thanked him for keeping Big Red when her father sold him to the ranch.

"My dear, I couldn't sell him when I saw how much you loved him. I thought if I kept him you might find a way to buy him back. I am so glad you have him again. He is a great horse. He has sired some great horses and I was glad I kept him."

The men got in the trailer and pushed the wagon out. They put the horses in the corral near the barn. When they got the wagon out Cookie came over to look it over. Jackson introduced him to Jasper and the two of them went in to see what he might still need to have it ready on Monday.

Cookie was surprised when he found out it had a propane stove and refrigerator in it. He could bring steaks with him to cook for the men. They all went in the house to go over the evening schedule for the youth. They would be coming in an hour.

Jackson told them what he planned for the classes he would be holding on Friday evenings. Part of it would be about safety around the rodeo stock and the rest would be about what they were interested in for the horse show.

He showed them the presentations Barbara prepared for the classes on barrel racing, reining and cow horse reining classes. The rest of the children would meet with Ellen, Joyce and Beth for their classes. The men would be with them in the stable to help them take care of their horses.

"Jackson, I love what you are doing for the youth in the area. I would love to be a part of it. I would be happy to come on the weekends to help and also, I would like to help financially."

"Jasper, I would love it if you would help with their training when we start talking about the care of the rodeo livestock and how they are chosen."

"Jackson, I would be honored to help. I know you probably know as much about it as I do, but it would be an honor to be involved."

When the youth started arriving, they were split up into the classes they were most interested in. Jackson sent the ones wanting to be barrel racers to the office with Barbara. He held the reining class in the den. George took the cow horse reining class into the office at the bunk house.

They explained to them how important it was for their horses to change leads at their command and it was to be done so the judges couldn't see them give the command. If the horse didn't respond to the lead changes they would be penalized and they would not score high enough to win. The horse and rider needed to work as one.

They went over the patterns several times until the kids knew them well. When it was dinner time, they went in to eat. After dinner, they went out to the bon-fire to have devotions and have a sing along before it was time to settle in for the night.

When the youth settled down for the night the adults met in the den to talk about how they thought the night went.

They all agreed it was a great idea to do the Friday night session. They felt like the kids learned a lot and tomorrow when they take their horses in the arena, they will better understand what they are going to need to do. They all felt the diagrams on the computer helped. They would be handy for them to review until they have the patterns down where they can run them in their sleep.

Ellen told them the kids interested in landscaping were really interested in learning about the different plants and what areas they could and couldn't be grown in. They were excited about working on the landscaping in the front of the house. They worked on drawing a design for it.

"Ellen, we are looking forward to seeing what they come up with. I know it will be great. Let me know what you need and I will give you the money. I've been meaning to have you landscape it ever since I bought the ranch. It just didn't seem to be the right time. I guess this is the reason why."

When everyone left. Jackson took Jasper upstairs and showed him his room. When he came down, he noticed the light was on in the office. He went in and saw Barbara at the computer.

"Honey, shut it off for the night and I will walk you to your apartment. What were you doing on the computer this late at night? You don't have to work so hard you know. I hope I'm not a bad boss."

"I wasn't working on office stuff. I just thought of something I wanted to add to my class. I'm glad I did though, I got you to walk me home."

"Honey, I will walk you home every night. I love doing it and besides it gives me a chance to kiss you good-night." He gave her a kiss. Then he left to go home.

The next morning, when Jackson came down stairs he looked outside and saw two long tables with benches in front of the youth bunk houses. Cookie and Joyce were out there putting breakfast on them. He asked Joyce where they came from. She told him Cookie built them and told her he would be helping her fix meals for everyone on the weekends.

"Cookie, what do I owe you for the tables? Thank you so much for doing this and helping Joyce with the meals. You know it wasn't part of the deal when I hired you."

"Boss you don't owe me anything. You have given me a chance to make a little difference in the lives of these young people and you don't know how much it means to me."

Jackson thanked him again and wondered what his story was. There was a sadness about him he hadn't noticed before.

When everyone was seated Jackson asked Jeff to say the blessing. He was working this weekend. Jackson was going to be preaching Sunday morning at the Spanish Church. When breakfast was over, they all went to where they would be working.

When he got to the arena, he saw Tyler going through the pattern for the reining horse class. He thought to himself the boy was a great rider and always willing to help anyone who needed it. Bill and Rhonda have done a great job with him. He envied them having a son like him. He hoped someday he and Barbara will have a family.

Jackson saw Mark's police car pull up at the house. He decided he'd best see what was going on. When he got close to the car, he noticed a young boy in the back seat. Mark got out and came over to talk to him.

"Jackson, I have a boy in the car I think could really use your Youth Camp. He is a very disturbed young man and it is either he comes here or goes to Juvenile Hall. He hasn't gotten into anything really bad yet, but he is heading there unless someone takes an interest in him. His Dad is in prison and his mother doesn't want him. I was hoping maybe you might take him under your wing. I really don't want to see him put in Juvenile Hall. He just turned 11 and there are a lot of hard cases there."

"Bring him in and let me talk to him. I'll see what I think I can do for him."

Jackson called Jeff to come to the office. Jeff wondered what was going on. He saw the police car pull up. He walked over to the office and saw a young boy with Mark talking to Jackson. The boy looked mad, but he also looked scared.

"Hi Mark, who have you got here? You don't look too happy to be here young man."

"Jeff this is Marty Parker. He has a decision he needs to make. He can either come here or he can go to Juvenile Hall. He is still trying to make up his mind."

"Mark, maybe we need to be the ones to decide if we want him here. Maybe he isn't smart enough to learn anything we want to teach him."

Jackson wondered what Jeff was up to. He knew he dealt with kids more than he did so he kept quiet and watched to see how this played out.

"I am too smart enough to learn anything you can teach. I bet I know more than you do about a lot of things."

"Well I guess we won't find out because you don't know if you want to be here."

"I didn't say I didn't want to stay here. I'm still thinking about it. What have you got to offer me?"

"Who says we have to offer you anything. You need to decide what you can offer us. I think you need to go out to the kitchen with Ms. Joyce while we decide if we want you here. You can decide whether you want to be here."

Jeff called Joyce and asked her to take Marty into the kitchen and give him some milk and cookies while they talked. She took him by the hand led him out of the room.

Jeff looked at Mark and told him the boy has been abused. He saw it in his eyes. He has seen other children with the same look. The boy needed someone to care about him, but it wasn't going to be easy to get through to him.

"I think the camp will be good for him, but what about the rest of the week. You can't undo the damage done to him just on the weekends. Mark, what is the plan where he is concerned."

"Jeff the problem is he has been in too many foster homes and he never fits in. If there are other children, he causes all the problems he can just to be moved."

"So, we need to find a home where he will be the only child and get one on one attentions from the foster parents."

"If you take him for the weekend here at the ranch, I will try to find someplace for him while he is here."

"Mark, we will let him stay. Jeff, you will need to keep a close eye on him, especially around the horses."

Jeff told him he would be responsible for him while he was there.

Jeff left the room and went out to get Marty and take him out to the stable.

"Mark, I hope we can find someone before Monday to take him. I would hate to see him go to Juvenile Hall. I don't think it is the place for him."

"Me too, I don't think he is a bad boy. He's had a rough life and I don't think it will get any better unless we can help him."

Jackson went out to the stable to see how things were going. He saw Jeff and Marty brushing one of the horses. The boy seemed like a different boy from the one he'd seen in the house. He was being so gentle with the horse. Jackson knew the boy would never abuse an animal like he was abused.

Lora drove out to the ranch after she closed the office. She saw Jeff and a young boy brushing a horse. She'd never seen the boy before. When she approached the boy seemed to draw into himself and she wondered what was going on.

"Hi honey, who have we got here?

"Hi sweetheart, this is Marty. Marty this in my wife, Ms. Lora."

Lora held out her hand to shake his and he hid behind the horse. She asked him if he was okay. She just wanted to shake his hand and welcome him. He looked at her and came out. He shook her hand but she could feel him tremble. She looked at Jeff with a question in her eyes.

"Honey Marty is new here. He just got here a little while ago. He has been helping me brush Prince."

"Well Marty I am glad to see you and you are doing a great job brushing Prince. He seems to be really liking it."

Tyler came up on his horse and asked Marty if he would like to saddle Prince and ride with him around the arena. Marty looked at Jeff and then told him he didn't know how to ride. Tyler told him Prince is really gentle and he would teach him how to ride if he wanted to.

Marty looked at Jeff and he told him it was alright.

"Marty, it is fine. Tyler is a really good rider and can teach you."

Tyler got off his horse and took Marty's hand and told him to come with him and they would get a saddle and bridle for Prince. The boys walked off together.

"Jeff, what is going on with the boy? He looks to me like he has been abused by a woman before."

"I figured he'd been abused; I just didn't know by whom. I think it was probably his mother. Mark said his dad is in prison and his mother abandoned him. If he can't find someone to foster him, by Monday he will have to stay in juvenile hall during the week. I'm not sure what it will do to him."

"Jeff, what would we have to do to take him? We have been talking about maybe adopting. This would give us a chance to see how we could make it work. The boy needs someone who cares to spend some time with him. He will be in school while we work. I think we could make it work for him and us. What do you think?"

"Let's see how he adjusts today and tomorrow. We can spend time with him here and see how it goes. We will talk about it Sunday night after the bon-fire."

Jackson noticed Lora and Jeff talking after Tyler left with Marty. He hoped they were talking about the boy. He asked God to work things out for them and the boy. He has a feeling they were meant for each other.

When everyone came over for lunch, Marty came to the table where Jeff and Lora were.

"Mr. Jeff, Tyler told me I will be a good rider."

"Tyler is a good rider and he knows when someone will be good."

Jeff looked over at Lora and saw her smiling at Marty with such a loving look in her eyes he had a feeling they would be talking to Mark before the weekend was over.

Marty ran over to where the other kids were getting ready to eat. Tyler moved over for him to sit beside him. Jeff thought the boy has a very good and loving heart. He has taken Marty under his wing and he knew the boy would be okay.

"Bill, you and Rhonda should be very proud of Tyler. He has a heart of gold. He has taken Marty under his wing and giving him a good time. The little boy has been through a lot and he needs the attention."

"Jeff, we have always been proud of him. The older he gets the prouder we are. He is going to make a great veterinarian."

"Well if he decides against being a vet, he would make a tremendous doctor."

Jackson came over and told them if he was needed, he would be in his office. He needs to finish his sermon for tomorrow or he will be having to wing it.

Lora decided by Saturday evening she and Jeff needed to talk to Mark and plan for Marty to go home with them on Sunday. She would go to school with him on Monday and plan for him to walk to the clinic after school. They could make this work. If he couldn't walk there, then she would pick him up after school and bring him there. She went to find Jeff and tell him what she decided.

"Jeff, I think we should talk to Mark and see what needs to be done in order to take Marty home with us tomorrow night. What do you think of the idea?

"Honey I am all for it, but we need to ask Marty if it is what he wants."

They decided to wait and see what happens on Sunday before they talked to Marty and then they would talk to Mark about him.

Jackson came out for the evening devotions and sing along. Then he said he has to go back and finish his sermon. He would see them all in the morning.

The kids all started going to their bunk houses. Chad noticed Marty just sat there.

"Marty is something wrong?"

"I don't know what I am supposed to do."

Chad took his hand and told him his bed was ready for him in the bunk house and he would be staying there with them tonight. When they got inside Tyler told him his bunk was under his.

Marty smiled and got ready for bed. He thought about how he liked it here and didn't ever want to leave. He wondered what would happen to him tomorrow. He knew he was only supposed to be here for the weekend. He heard Mr. Mark talking to them about where he would go on Monday. He sure wished he could go home with Mr. Jeff and Ms. Lora They really seemed to like him and he really like them. He wasn't afraid of Ms. Lora; she wouldn't hurt him like his momma did. Mr. Jackson told them they could talk to God and he would help them. So maybe if I ask Him, he will let me go home with them.

"I don't know you God, but Mr. Jackson and Mr. Jeff say you know me. Would you please send me home with Mr. Jeff and Ms. Lora and I promise to be really good? Thank you, God."

On the way home Jeff told Lora he has a feeling God was wanting them to call Mark and see what they could do about bringing Marty home with them tomorrow until something more permanent could be arranged. She told him to go ahead and call. She felt as strong about it as he did.

"Hi Mark, what would Lora and I need to do in order to bring Marty home with us tomorrow until we can get licensed to be foster parents?"

"I had a feeling you would be calling me. I saw how the boy related to you. I will talk to the Judge tomorrow at Church and get the okay. I will drop off the paper work for you to become his foster parents at your office on Monday. I really believe all he needs is to be loved."

"I think you are right. You should have seen how well he got along with everyone today. He was like a different person when I got him around the horses. He was afraid of Lora when she first came. She reached out to shake his hand and he hid behind the horse. I'm sure his mother was the one abusing him."

"I'm pretty sure you're right. He cringes every time his mother is mentioned."

"Thanks for your help Mark and we will see you in Church tomorrow. Jackson is preaching at the Spanish Church."

The next morning, everyone went to breakfast and then got ready to leave for Church. Jeff and Lora pulled up and said, "Marty come with us we brought you clothes to wear to Church."

They took him in the house to change. He came out of the bathroom smiling. He told them he never had anything nice before.

Jackson came in and told him he looked really nice. He was glad he was coming to Church with Mr. Jeff and Ms. Lora.

Jeff took Jackson aside and told him what they were planning on doing. He said he knew it yesterday when he met the boy. He saw it in his eyes when he looked at him. He told him it would be nice to have another nephew to spoil.

They all left for Church. Some of them went to the Methodist Church, some to the Community Christian Church and Jackson and four of the Mexican boys went to the Spanish Church.

When Church was over, they all headed back to the ranch. Marty had ridden with Jeff and Lora. Jeff told him they wanted to talk to him about something. They asked him what he thought about coming home with them until they could get permission from the state to keep him. He told them God did listen to him and then he just smiled.

Lora thought she was going to really enjoy having this little boy around. She hoped everything will work out and maybe they will someday be able to adopt him.

"Jeff, the Judge okayed everything and he saw no reason you couldn't be appointed his foster parents. He said to fill out the paper work and get it to him tomorrow and he will sign it. Lora, it helps to have friends in high places. It normally takes months to get it done."

Jackson came over to where they were talking and heard the last part. He gave Marty a hug and told him he liked having another nephew. Marty smiled and hugged him back.

"Mr. Jackson, you told me God would listen to me and I asked Him to let me live with Mr. Jeff and Ms. Lora and He did."

Jackson said thank you God under his breath. You are an awesome God always.

Jackson had given his sermon on the different meanings of Love. He told God he was seeing the true meaning of love right now in His brother, sister-in-law and the little boy who needed someone to love him so badly.

"Barb, how do you think the weekend went?"

"It went great. The best part of it was Jeff and Lora leaving tonight with Marty to take him home with them."

"I agree with you totally. I knew the minute Jeff met him it was going to happen. Lora and Jeff can't have children and I have a feeling they will be filling their home with a lot of children who need their love just like our parents did."

"If something happens and we can't have children of our own I would be just as happy adopting. I don't know how people can turn their backs on a child."

"Jackson, I know what you mean. Sometimes I wonder if I have what caused my mother to hemorrhage when she had me. Someday I will talk to a doctor about it. I would hate to leave a baby for someone else to raise. I want to see my children grow up."

"Honey, I am sure if your mother gave birth in a hospital, she would be here with you today. You can't worry about things before they happen. Yes, you should get checked over before we have children for your own peace of mind, but I don't want you worrying about it."

"I need to let you go to bed. You have to be up early tomorrow to get ready for the round-up. The boys all spent the night so they would be here in the morning. I think they were afraid you might leave without them."

"I will get enough sleep. I want to spend a few more minutes just holding you. Okay with you?"

"It's more than okay with me. I will miss you while you are gone. Please come home as fast as you can and be careful. Those cattle haven't seen humans and horses in a long time."

They sat quietly for another hour and then Jackson walked her over to her apartment and kissed her good-night.

He went to bed thanking God for the wonderful day they had. He was happy for his brother, Lora and Marty. He knew it was all God's doing. He went to bed thinking maybe it was time to ask Barbara to marry him. He asked God to let him know when it is time.

Chapter Eight

Monday morning everyone met in the kitchen to have breakfast and talk about the round-up.

Jackson told them where the cattle were located and they should be able to get to the area by early afternoon.

"I want to set up a camp before we get there. Then ride to where the cattle are. I want to see how they react to the horses and men. They have been on open range for over two years. They won't be use to horses or people. We will camp for the night and then get them gathered for the trip back to the ranch."

Davis told them they would need to be sure none of them separated from the herd.

"We will work in teams and each team will have an area to watch. We all need to be careful not to spook them. One bull running scared could start a stampede. They will be hard to stop if they start running."

When the men from the other ranches arrived, they all divided into teams so they knew who they were working with. They divided the four boys each with a different group.

"Mark when we get close, I want you to ride out with me to see if there are any health problems. I don't want to take a chance of caring any disease to the livestock at the ranch."

They all went out to get their horses saddled and got ready to leave. Jackson went in the office to tell Barb they should be back in a couple of days if everything goes alright.

They stopped for lunch and Cookie had sandwiches made for them. When they were done Jackson looked at the map to see how close they were getting. He told them they would be setting up camp in a couple of hours. Then he would take four of the men with him to check on the cattle and decide how to work them.

"Tyler, you will have to control Spirit. He is a cutting horse and will tend to want to cut them out of the herd. Just keep a tight hand on him."

Later in the day they knew they were getting close to where they saw them. He had Cookie and Jasper set up camp. Then he took four of the men with him to go see if they were still in the area.

When they found them Jackson said, "Davis there seems to be some missing. We will need to look in the wooded area to see if any are in there."

Davis and two of the others went into the woods to look for them. Jackson and Mark went back toward the mountain range. They found an opening in the mountain and decided to take a look.

When they got through, they found a meadow and the rest of the herd there grazing.

"We might have a problem trying to drive them back through the opening. I do notice though they don't seem to mind us or our horses. It will make it a little easier. We need to get Davis and see if we can find a way to close the opening. It would be

108

better to get them back on this side tonight rather than come out here tomorrow and find the whole herd in there."

When they got back to the rest of the herd, Davis was just coming back from checking the woods.

"Davis, we found the rest of the herd on the other side of the mountain."

"Jackson, we can probably find some logs to block the entrance."

They sent Phil back to get the rest of the men to help.

Mark rode in closer to the herd to see if he could see any health problems. When he rode back, he told Jackson they all looked healthy.

Jackson told Davis and Mark something didn't seem right about this.

"Don't you think this herd is awfully calm about us being around them. They have supposedly been out here for over two years with no human contact."

"It does seem strange. What are you thinking? Do you think someone has been out here around them.?"

"I think we need to take a ride before we run them back through the opening."

When they rode back to the meadow, they saw a house in the distance. Jackson decided to go talk to whoever owned it.

"Maybe this is the reason for the herd being so calm. The owner of the house may own part of the cattle. I know there are more than I expected out here."

They rode down to the house. A young boy ran out to the barn calling for his father. When the man came out of the barn, he had a rifle in his hand.

"You don't need the rifle. I just need to talk to you about the cattle in the meadow."

"Why do you want to know about my cattle? Where did you come from anyway?"

"I'm Jackson Barnes and I own the 1000 acres on the other side of the mountain range. I came looking for the cattle the man I bought the ranch from told me were out here somewhere. I spotted them last week from an airplane and came to round them up and take them back to the ranch. The thing is I need to know how many belong to you."

"My name is Lawrence Patterson but I go by Larry. As far as the cattle are concerned, I guess they really belong to you. They just showed up and when no one came to claim them after six months I started using them to make a living for me and my family. I have sold some and have butchered some for food."

"Well, Larry I tell you what, why don't you take a ride with us to the meadow and we will see what we can do to make sure you still have the means to take care of your family."

"I don't understand, they belong to you. I've delivered a couple of the calves over the years, but otherwise they have lived off the grass and water in the area."

"Let me put it this way. You were honest with me. You could have told me half of them were yours and I wouldn't have known the difference. I don't plan on making my living off them. I raise rodeo livestock and horses. I also run the Youth Camp at the ranch. I want you and your family to continue having an income to live on."

"I've heard about the Youth Camp. My son's been wanting to go, but I can't afford anything else right now."

"Your son is welcome to come anytime and the camp is free. We don't charge for it. It is just something the Lord put on my heart to do and everyone volunteers."

"Wait a minute, your Jackson Barnes the rodeo star and preacher I've heard so much about."

"I'm just a rancher and part-time preacher now. Let's go look at those cattle before they decide it's time to go back on the other side."

They went back to the meadow and looked at the herd. There was an older bull and a young bull plus 8 cows with calves in the meadow. "Larry will they make a good start for you?"

"Jackson, it sure would and I will be glad to pay for them as soon as I can."

"You don't owe me anything and bring your son to the ranch next weekend. The youth come on Friday evening and stay until Sunday night. You're free to come and see what we do and maybe I can talk you into volunteering some time. We will close off the opening in the mountain wall for now so the cattle can't come and join the ones we will be driving to the ranch tomorrow."

When they got back on the other side the men had logs to close off the entrance. Jackson told them to go ahead and close it. They wouldn't be bringing the other cattle through.

Davis thought to himself, he couldn't believe there was someone like Jackson in this world. He not only preached about kindness, but he sure lived it. How many men would give up a herd of expensive cattle. He wouldn't have believed it if he hadn't seen it with his own eyes.

When they got back to camp, he told the others he didn't think they would have any problem moving the cattle.

"They are very docile. We just need to take it slow and easy. We should be back home tomorrow evening."

Jackson thought even with what he gave to Larry he still has a good size herd of angus cattle to take back to the ranch.

He wasn't sure he wanted to raise them, but he owned them. A good black angus steak sounded really good about now.

"Cookie you and Jasper can head out after breakfast. Stop around noon and fix lunch. Then you can head back to the ranch and we will eat dinner when we get there."

The next morning the men had already taken their positions around the cattle and were ready to move them out. It took the cattle a while to get used to being herded. Eventually they started going in the direction they were driving them. Once in a while one would try to break out. Spirit and Tyler would get it back in before any others could start following. Jackson watched the boy and horse work and thought he was one great wrangler.

By noon they were up to the chuck wagon. Cookie and Jasper had hamburgers, baked beans and ice tea ready for them. The cattle seemed to be content to just graze while they ate. When they were done Cookie and Jasper left for the ranch.

They got the cattle moving again and started their last part of the trip. They took their time and the cattle seemed content to just keep moving at a slow pace. By late afternoon they could see the pasture where they were going to put them. The cattle walked into the pasture and Jackson and Davis got off their horses and closed the gates and locked them.

"You go to the ranch and wash up for dinner. Cookie will have dinner ready for you by the time you get there."

When Jackson got there the women were setting the food on the long tables by the bunk houses. Cookie and Joyce were cooking steaks for everyone.

Barbara saw him ride up and came to the stable to meet him. He gave her a sweet kiss and told her he was sorry for kissing her when he was so dirty. She laughed and told him she didn't care. She missed him.

Jackson took care of his horse and then went to the wash room to clean up before going to eat. They went out to the table and Jackson said the blessing and thanked God for their round-up and the food they were about to eat.

The boys were talking about the round-up and how great it was. Tyler told everyone how great Spirit worked the cattle. Jackson and the others smiled at each other and told everyone they were all four great wranglers and would be happy to have them work with them anytime.

"I am going to have Ms. Barbara put the film on a DVD for you to take to school. The principle wants you to tell the assembly on Friday about your experience on the round-up."

"Jackson, in all of my 70 years I have not had as much fun as I've had the last two days. I think when I sell my ranch, I will look for a place here in Hidden Valley. I really like it here and love how the people all seem to take everyone into their hearts."

"Jasper, we would love for you to move here. When you get the ranch sold you are welcome to stay here on the ranch with us until you find someplace you would like to buy. We would love to have you."

"Jackson, I never had children but I feel like I found a son in you. My wife died very young and I never found anyone I could love as much as I loved her. Don't waste your time with Barbara on whatever you feel is a problem. Life is too short to have regrets."

"Thank you, Jasper. I know you are right and I have already decided nothing matters except we love each other. God will help us work the rest of it out."

The men from the other ranches loaded their horses and headed for home. Everyone was tired and needed a bath and a good night's sleep. Jackson went in to take a shower and then he went to talk to Barbara. She was in the office putting the pictures from the round-up on the DVD for the boys. He walked over to her and took her hand.

"Barb, I have been doing a lot of thinking and I know I love you and want you to be my wife. I know we said we wanted to take it slow and we will, but would you please wear my ring. When you are ready, we will plan a wedding, but not before. I need to know you will be my wife someday soon."

"Oh, Jackson I would be honored to wear your ring. I love you with all my heart. I want to be your wife. I promise we will be married soon."

"This ring is the one I bought you 4 years ago. We can pick out a different one later if you want."

"Jackson, this one is perfect. I love it and wouldn't want anything else."

He put the ring on her finger and gave her a long and sweet kiss. They stood there in each other's arms for a long time. He thought how good she felt in his arms. He knew God picked her out for him years ago. They just needed this time to get to know each other better.

Barbara couldn't believe she and Jackson were finally going to be husband and wife. She dreamed of this day for so long. She thanked God for giving them to each other.

The next morning when they came in for breakfast, Jackson gave her a sweet kiss and told the others he asked Barbara to marry him and she said yes.

"Well, big brother it is about time you came to your senses. I knew the first time I saw the two of you in the same room you loved each other. I began to think you had lost your mind."

Everyone congratulated them and asked when the wedding would be. Barbara told them they hadn't talked about a date yet. She told them she hoped it would be before too long though.

"We need to get Cal and Gloria married first and then Meredith and Brad. Then we will set a date for ours. This is going to be a busy year for weddings in the family I guess."

"Well brother, maybe we should have a triple wedding and get it all over with at once."

"Cal, I'm not sure your bride or our sister would be okay with that. I think we need to stick to three separate weddings. Besides I don't intend to rush Barb. She is the one who will set the date."

Barbara and Jackson went to the office to work. He wanted to go through the previous owner's records. He wanted to see what was there concerning the herd he brought back to the ranch. He knew from looking at them they were from good stock.

Barbara finished the DVD and told Jackson it was ready for the boys to take to school with them on Friday. He told her he would get it to Zack to take with him.

She came in the file room to help him with the records. She said, "there is a buyer coming this week to look at the herd and see if he wanted any of them."

"Barb have you thought about barrel racing at some of the rodeos I will be taking livestock too? I want you with me when I go and you might as well ride while we are there."

"Jackson, I don't know if I am good enough anymore. It has been four years since I rode in a rodeo."

"Honey, I watch you every day working with Red. You and the horse are as good now as you were back then. We have a rodeo coming up in two weeks. It is in Raleigh, North Carolina. We can get you registered next week. Just think about it, okay?"

"Jackson, what about the camp weekend. You have the men to take over for you, but who will work with the barrel racers?"

"Barb, you have two of the older girls who are really good. I have been watching them work. You can show one of them or both what you want the others to work on and let them take care of it. You have a weekend you can work with them so they can take over for one weekend. Maybe the next time we can arrange for the barrel racers to go with us to watch you ride."

"Okay, I will think about it. I really do miss the rodeo and riding. Red is ready for sure. I just have to get my confidence back."

Jackson found the previous owners records and as he looked at them, he saw the cattle came from one of the best breeding stocks in the country. He also saw he was making a good living with them until his wife died. Then he quit selling them and just seemed to give up on the ranch. No wonder he didn't try to find the ones at the end of the ranch. He sold what he found and then got out of the business.

"Jackson, if something ever happens to me you better not give up on life. He didn't honor his wife by giving up on himself. No wife would want her husband to give up and neither would God."

"Barb, I remember the situation. He sold everything to pay her medical bills and wanted to make a new start. He seemed to be having a real hard time adjusting."

They decided to hold hands and pray he was adjusting to his new life and the pain was lessoning. He prayed for God to hold him in his loving arms and heal him.

"Honey, I need to go check on the herd and see what I want to keep. The first buyer will be here this afternoon. I need to have an idea of what I am doing. I'll see you at lunch. Make some copies of these papers about the cattle's breeding to give to the buyers."

"Jackson, Mark said the cattle are all in good health. The open range has been good for them. They are a great looking bunch of Angus cattle."

"Davis, we need to decide what we want to keep. There is a buyer coming this afternoon to look them over and another one tomorrow."

Davis told him there was a couple of exceptional bulls in the group. They were young and well built. They would be good for breeding. Any of the cows would make good breeding stock. They all have calves by their side so any of them would be a good choice to keep.

"Well let's see what the buyers want and then we will decide what we are going to do. Separate the two bulls from them and put them in the corral. I do know I want to send two of the cows to the processing plant for meat this winter. We will need to pick them out and send them before Barb decides to make pets out of them."

Barb came out to the pasture to give Jackson the paperwork she copied for him and told him the buyer called from town and was on his way out.

"Jackson, look what sweet faces they have. They are so beautiful. Look at all the babies."

"Barb, go back to the house. We are not going to make pets out of any of them. I know they are beautiful, but they are cows not puppy dogs, okay."

She laughed as she walked away. She hollered back she knew what they were. She was a ranch girl not a city slicker. She knew what they were raised for.

Jackson shook his head and told Davis she never failed to amaze him. They started looking over the cattle to see if there was any they didn't want to sell.

The buyer showed up and Jackson went over to talk to him. He told him the cattle had been on open range for over two years and had not been grained. They had no hormones given to them or antibiotics. They were strictly grass fed.

"This is what I am looking for. I have two restaurants where we sell the best steaks in the country. We only buy good beef free of any type of foreign substance. Jackson, I hope we can continue doing business. I like what I've seen."

He looked over the cattle and tagged the ones he wanted to buy. They settled on a price and Jackson told him they would deliver them the next day.

When he went to the office, he gave Barb the check for the cattle.

"Maybe you should consider keeping the cattle as a second income for the ranch."

"Honey, we have to deliver the ones he bought tomorrow. They have to go to Kentucky so we will be gone a couple of days."

"Jackson, what about the buyer coming tomorrow? Should I call him and put him off for a couple of days?"

"No, I'll send Davis and Chad to deliver this bunch and be here for the buyer. I'm really not anxious to be away from you so soon anyway."

"Davis, I need you and Chad to deliver the cattle. I have another buyer coming out in the morning."

"Jackson, we will get them separated and ready to load in the morning."

Jasper came out of the house and asked Jackson if he could help with anything.

"Jasper, would you mind staying a few more days until Davis gets back from delivering the cattle. I will have him take You, the wagon and draft horses' home then."

"Jackson, I don't mind at all. I called the ranch and everything is fine there. Jackson, I want you to keep the wagon and draft horses. I don't use them anymore. We used them for the parade on opening day of the rodeo."

"Jasper, I would love to buy them, but right now I need to see how the rodeos go and the sale of the cattle before I buy anything else."

Jackson, I don't want to sell them to you. I am giving them to you. I don't have any need for them anymore and I want them to go to someone who will take good care of them."

"Well thank you and I do hope you will come stay with us when you get your ranch sold. I feel like you are a very special friend and I thank God he sent me to you when I was looking for the rodeo livestock."

Jackson went to help Davis and the men separate the cattle he sold. They put them in the corral so they could load them in the morning.

After dinner Jackson asked, "Barb would you like to go to the den and have devotions with me. I want to always keep the Lord in our lives and I can't think of a better way than doing our devotions together."

"Jackson, nothing would make me happier than to do them together."

They went in the den. They both thanked God for what he was doing in their lives. They promised they would always rely on Him no matter what the future brings in to their lives. He would always be first.

"Barb, now we know we want to be together, don't make me wait too long to be married. I know I told you I wouldn't rush you and I don't mean to. I love you and want you to be my wife."

"Jackson, do we have to wait for Cal and Gloria to be married? We don't know when Meredith plans to have her wedding, but we do know Cal and Gloria want to wait until the house is finished in the spring."

"Honey, we could be married tomorrow and I would be happy. I want you to have a beautiful wedding. You deserve to have one."

"Jackson, I don't want a big wedding. I have no family of my own, so I don't have to worry about who I would need to invite. It is up to you if you want a big one. I would be happy with just family and a few close friends being there."

"Honey, I don't need a big wedding either. I do want to see you in a wedding dress though. We can have a small wedding and then have a reception everyone can come to. We will talk about all of it later, when you decide on a date. Now I am going to walk you to your apartment."

When they got to the apartment, he kissed her good-night and told her he would see her in the morning.

Barbara got to thinking, while she was getting ready for bed, maybe a Christmas wedding would be nice. They could have it in the house. They could decide what they wanted to do to the house and fix it up nice. She would have to think about it.

The next morning after breakfast Jackson went to help Davis and Chad load the cattle to deliver to the buyer. When he came back to the office Barb asked him what he'd been thinking when he mentioned doing some different things to the house.

"When the buyer leaves this morning, maybe we could go look the house over and see what you think needs to be done to make it ours."

When the buyer came. Jackson took him out to see the herd. When he found out they were all raised on open range he was anxious to buy as many as he could. Jackson told him he wasn't interested in getting rid of a large number as he decided to increase his herd.

They made a deal with his right to buy from him every few months. Jackson told him it would be a couple of days before he could deliver them as his foreman was delivering some right now and would be home tomorrow.

He took the check into Barb and told her of the deal he made with the buyer. She told him he made the right decision. The Angus cattle will help keep the ranch going until the rodeo livestock starts making enough to keep the ranch out of the red.

Chapter Nine

After lunch Jackson and Barbara went upstairs to look at the bedrooms. Barb couldn't believe what she saw. There were two master suites with their own bath rooms and walk-in-closets. Two large bedrooms with a large bathroom between them. There was also a long room at the top of the stairs open to the living room and den below. It has a beautiful railing matching the stairway going up to them.

"Jackson, I love it. We only need to paint and have new carpet put in. The only other thing would be new curtains and bedspreads. The furniture in the rooms is beautiful and good quality. We could do one room at a time."

"Honey, we need to do the two master suites right away. If Jasper sells his ranch and comes here until he finds a place, I want to have one ready for him. When we get married Joyce and George will move out to your apartment. Right now, they use one of the bedrooms and the balcony area for their living room."

"When I pick out the curtains and bed spreads for the master suites, I will keep Jasper in mind. I hope he does get the ranch sold and comes here. I don't like the idea of him being there alone now the men all work here."

"He still has one ranch hand and his cook living there with him. But I would like him to be here with us. He has become more like family."

They went downstairs to look at everything. She asked him if he has any special plans for the downstairs.

"I want to open up the family room and den into one large room. I want to put in French doors going out the back of the house and put in a large patio outside facing the mountains."

"Jackson, I love it. If we get it done before we get married, I would love to be married here with the view of the mountains in the background."

"I will talk to Don and see when he can schedule it. He has the stable and Cal's house right now. I will see if he can work it in as soon as the stable is done."

"Barb, what do you think about building an office and turning this office back into a master suite? I thought we could build it at the end of the driveway. We have so many strangers coming to see the cattle. I want to hire someone to work with you. He or she would be your assistant. When you are with me at the rodeo, you wouldn't be swamped when you get back."

"Jackson, it would be great, but you would have to be very careful who you hire. I handle a lot of money and the wrong person could cause you a lot of trouble."

"You will do all the interviews and we will have Tom do a thorough background search. Whoever we hire will work for you. You will have the last say and how much you let the handle will be up to you.

Jackson and Barb talked about all of his business accounts and how to separate them.

"Barb, I want you to set up a program for my personal accounts and monitor them for me. I am really not sure what I have and what my investments are doing. I had money invested when I was with the rodeo and forgot about it. I got a notice from them wanting to know if I wanted to reinvest part of it somewhere else."

"Jackson, bring me everything you have and let me go over them. I will set you up a program on the computer to tract them."

"Here are the security codes to all of my accounts. When I get in them, I am lost. I am not good with numbers. I just know I'm not broke."

"You are hopeless. I need to go over all of them and see where you stand. Your business accounts are good so I have time to go over your personal accounts with you."

"The work we do on the house will come out of my personal account. The new office will be a business cost. When we know how much I have in the personal accounts we will talk to Don and have him start on the work in the house first. Then I will have him see about the office building."

"Jackson, give me the notice they sent you. You probably don't have the account on your computer. I will set everything up so you know exactly what you have and where. When I have it straightened out, you may want to have Tom check on your investments. He works with investments all the time and handles them for Hank and for Hank's wife's estate."

"Okay, let me know when you have them ready. We will take them to Tom. Have I told you today I love you?"

"I love you to. You'll never know just how much. I don't want to wait too long to get married. I decided I will go with you to the rodeo in North Carolina and ride. Please don't expect too much out of me though."

"You will do great. You have a great horse and you are an exceptional rider. I am so glad you decided to do this. I know how much you have missed it."

"Barb, let's go into town and pick up some paint samples for the house. We have time before dinner. Anything in the office can wait until tomorrow."

They went to town and picked up the paint samples at the hardware store. As they were walking out, they ran into Don.

"Don, I need to talk to you about some jobs I want you to do for me."

"Well let's go have a cup of coffee and talk while I have a few minutes."

"We have plenty of time right now. We just came in to pick up some paint samples."

Jackson told Don what he wanted to do in the house and to build a separate office for the ranch. He wanted to turn the office back into a master suite like it was before the previous owner made it an office.

"Jackson, I will be done with the new stable in about a week. I could start on whatever you want then."

"Don, I thought I wanted to do the house first but now I think I would like to get the office built first. When we start on the house, we can do it all and not have you come back for the master bedroom."

"Have you talked to Brad about a plan for the office? I will need him to draw you a plan and have your approval. If the weather holds, we could probably get the foundation in and get it in the dry before bad weather."

"I will go over and talk to him now and see if he can get it done for you. It won't be too complicated. It will need two office spaces and a bathroom."

When they finished their coffee, they went over to Brad's office to talk to him. They explained to him what they wanted and Barb told him what needed to be in the building. She said it needed to have two offices, a rest room, a reception area and a room for the printers, fax machines and file cabinets.

He asked Jackson how big he wanted the building to be and Jackson asked him to determine what size it should be for all their needs.

"Let me know when you have the plans and I will come and approve them. Just be sure it is wired for everything they need and for a security system."

"Jackson, I will have the plans for you in a few days. I think you are smart to get your office outside of your house. You have a lot going on with the cattle and the rodeo livestock. Have you talked to Meredith lately? She has set our wedding for the first weekend in May. I know she is planning to ask you to give her away."

"No, I haven't talked to her in a while. I'm glad to know when it is though. I will be honored to give her away. I have asked Barbara to marry me and we are trying to decide when to plan our wedding. It is going to be a busy year for weddings in our family. I know Cal and Gloria are just waiting to find out when their house will be done to set their wedding date."

"Barb, are you alright with having the office done first. I should have asked you before I decided. If you don't want to do it this way, I will have Don do the house first and take care of the master suite down stairs later."

"Jackson, whatever you think is best is fine with me. I will plan our wedding when we know the house will be ready or we can be married in the Church."

"Honey, the reason I decided on the office is because winter will be here, before it can be built. I really don't want people coming in the house during the winter to take care of business."

"Jackson, I agree it will be better to have the separate office by then. We are planning on a small wedding and we could still have it in the house even if we don't get the rooms enlarged."

"Honey, I want you to have the kind of wedding you want. Hopefully Don can get the office situated so he can work on opening the two rooms in the house too."

They went home to have dinner. When the men came in to eat, he said the blessing and then told them of his plan to have an office built. They all thought it was a good idea.

He told Barb to get an ad in the paper for an assistant. He wanted to hire someone as soon as they could.

Joyce told him it was about time he got her help.

"Barb will be going with me to the rodeo in two weeks. She is going to enter barrel racing again."

Jasper said he was happy for her. He loved to watch her and Big Red. They were a winning team. Everyone said she would come home a winner.

"Please don't expect too much. I haven't ridden in a rodeo in four years. There are a lot of young, good riders out there now."

After dinner, Jackson and Barb went in the den to talk. Jackson noticed a car pull up in front of the house. He went to answer the door and saw Meredith and Brad walk up on the porch.

"Meredith, where is Shane? I haven't seen him in a while."

"He is with his Grandpa Don. Those two are inseparable when Don is home."

"What do I owe to this visit from my baby sister? It is very seldom I get to see you anymore."

"Well, it is Bill and Tom's fault they keep me busy at the law office. I came to ask you if you would give me away at my wedding. You fathered me and Cal all our lives. I figured it would be a chance to get even with you."

"Sis, I would be honored to fill in for Dad. I know he would be proud of you if he were here today."

"Thank you. Jackson, you don't know how much it means to me. I love you, big brother. So, what is this I hear about you two finally deciding to quit playing games and get married? I've been wondering if you would ever come to your senses. All we need is for Beth to decide to get serious about Pat and we will have the whole family taken care of."

Joyce came in with coffee and cake. She told Jackson she was going upstairs now. He thanked her and told her they would clean up before they went to bed.

"Jackson, after you left, I drew a plan for your office. If you like it, I will do the drawings for Dad and he can start lining up a crew for the work."

"Hey, it is great. Say can you look at this wall for me and tell me if we can take it out. I want to open up this room into the family room. Then I want to put French doors where those two large windows are in the family room."

"Jackson, it is a load bearing wall. We could put in the large timbers like we did in Bill's house and it would work. We may have to put in one column in the middle of the room. Or we could put in two columns and make it look like it was meant to be."

"Brad draw up something giving us an idea of what it will look like."

"I will do it first thing in the morning while I'm working on the final plans for the office."

Barbara was listening to them talk and thought how wonderful it was going to be when she was part of this wonderful family.

"Meredith would you be my maid-of-honor? I have no family and I would love it if you would."

"Barb, I would be honored to. You know you do have family a very large and noisy family."

Meredith gave her a hug and told her they were glad to have her in the family.

"Thank you, you don't know how much it means to me."

When Meredith and Brad left, Jackson and Barbara went out to clean the kitchen. When they were done, they went back in the den to do their devotions. Later Jackson walked her to her apartment and gave her a kiss good-night.

"Honey, I will be glad when we're married. Now we've

decided we belong together it seems like forever before we can say I do."

"Jackson, I promise you it won't be long. What would you think about getting married between Christmas and the first of the year? If the house isn't ready, we can still be married in the living room. We are planning a small wedding anyway."

The next morning when Jackson came downstairs, Barbara was already in the kitchen talking to Joyce What are you doing up so early? You don't have to be in the office for another two hours,"

"I was awake and wanted to have breakfast with you before you go to work. Who is delivering the other cattle to the buyer this morning?"

"Chad and John are taking them. They should be back by chore time tonight. I was just going out to help load them. The men separated them out yesterday."

"I forgot to tell you; I had a call yesterday as soon as the ad came out for an assistant. She is coming this morning to talk to me. I will have Tom check her out if I think she will work. I would prefer to have another woman in the office with me."

"I agree with you. I think it would be easier for you to work with another woman in such small quarters. Honey you do the interview. It is up to you who we hire for the job."

"I still would like you to be there if you can. I will do the hiring but I still want to know what you think of her."

"I will be in when we get the men on the way with the cattle. I always want to be there for you."

When the woman came Barbara noticed she was probably at least 15 years older than she was. She introduced herself as Marisa Moreno.

"I have worked for the same company for the last 15 years. They were just sold to a larger company and they want to bring in their own employees. They have let half of the staff go. I like working for smaller businesses and I was raised on a farm. I know something about cattle and horses. When I was young, I kept the books for the farm."

"Marisa, how will you feel about working for someone younger than you? I know with your experience you may not want to take orders from me."

"It would not be a problem. I like the idea of someone else having the responsibility now. I have been doing it too many years."

"Our bookkeeping and accounting here are a little more complicated. We have four different businesses to keep up with. We have one for the rodeo livestock, one for the Black Angus cattle, one for the ranch itself and one for the Youth Camp Jackson and Cal run. They are talking about maybe adding another enterprise. Would any of it be a problem for you?"

"Wow, girl you must be a whiz kid if you keep everything straight. I'm sure you can teach me whatever I need to know. I do know a lot about setting up accounting programs so maybe I can be of help."

Jackson came in as they were talking. He liked the looks and sound of the lady talking to Barb. He went over and introduced himself and shook her hand.

"Well how are you ladies coming along? From what I heard when I walked in, I think you are doing fine. How long have you been out of work Marisa?"

"My last day with the company was yesterday. I saw your ad as I was cleaning out my desk. I felt like it was God telling me to come here."

"Well the office is Barbara's domain, so whatever she decides is up to her. I will leave you ladies to your conversation. Barbara can I speak to you a minute. Marisa, it was very nice to meet you."

When they left the office, Jackson asked Barb what she thought about Marisa.

"I am going to hire her if her background check is okay. I think we will work well together."

131

"I think you're right. I can tell she is a Christian. Call Tom and tell him to rush the search. Love you and see you later. I will tell Joyce to bring you ladies some coffee and cookies."

A few minutes later Joyce came in with the coffee and cookies. Barb introduced her to Marisa. The ladies shook hands and Marisa thanked her for the coffee and cookies.

Joyce smiled at Barbara and told her she liked this lady and then she left the room.

"Marisa, I will need to have a background check done. Not only because of the accounting job, but because it is required of anyone who works on the ranch when the kids are here. They only come on the weekends during the school year. They are here every day in the summer. Will it present a problem for you? I will be out of the office a lot in the summer as I teach barrel racing."

"It will not be a problem. I love children and wouldn't mind working with them too."

"When will you be ready to start work? I will have Tom put a rush on your background check."

"I can start whenever you are ready for me. I look forward to working with you and I would like to know more about the Youth Camp. I have no family close and would love to have something to be involved in on the weekends."

"I will call Tom now and you can start tomorrow. It doesn't take him long to get things done. He is a retired JAG officer and still has lots of government contacts."

"I will be here at 8:30 in the morning then. I look forward to working with you and I have a great feeling about this. I think God has his hand in it."

"I have no doubts about it. You will find this valley is very special. God has his hands on it all the time."

Barbara called Tom and gave him Marisa's information and told him she needed the report ASAP. She told him she was starting tomorrow morning.

Tom called back an hour later. "Barbara, I have your report on Marisa. She has a great work record. She is a widow. She lost her son and husband in a car accident 10 years ago. She is a member of the First United Methodist Church in Roanoke and is active with the youth group there."

She thanked Tom and told him to give her love to his family. She was glad Marisa checked out. She looked forward to working with her.

Barbara went in the kitchen to get a glass of ice tea. "Joyce, Marisa will be starting in the morning. She works with the youth at her Church in Roanoke."

She didn't tell her about losing her son and husband. It is Marisa's story to tell.

"Barbara, I liked her the minute I met her. I think you are a good fit."

Jackson came in and Barbara told him she would like to talk to him in the office for a minute.

He told her he would be right in as soon as he cleaned up a little. He had been working with the cattle.

"Hi Honey, what is up. Did you hire Marisa? I think she will be just what you need in the office."

"Yes, I did and Tom has already given the okay. She is a youth leader in her Church in Roanoke. He also told me she is a widow. She lost her husband and son in a car accident 10 years ago. She is interested in working with the Youth camp here."

"That is great, I think the two of you will work great together.

"Jackson, what do you think about getting married on the 29th of December. It will be the Friday after Christmas. If the house isn't done by then we can be married in the living room. I only want your family and our closest friends here. I thought we could have Cookie and Joyce prepare a BBQ on Saturday for everyone."

"Honey it sounds great to me. If Don gets the office in the dry, we can have him put it on hold long enough to take out the wall and put in the French doors. We will get a painter in to paint the upstairs and the rest of the house right away. Then there won't be much to do when the wall comes out."

Jackson called Brad to see how things are going.

"Brad, have you given the plans to your father?"

"Dad has the plans and intends to have the foundation in this week. I also have the drawings for you of the room when the wall is taken out."

"Barb and I will be in today to look at them. Barb, we are going to take a ride to town. Brad says he has the drawings of the wall ready for us to look at."

"Okay, I'll shut down the computer and be ready to go in a couple of minutes. I'll meet you at the car."

She saved the work she was doing and went to get her coat and meet him.

"Joyce, we are going to have dinner in town." She told them to have a good time.

When they got there, Brad showed them what he thought they should do. The picture showed a large open beam made of the same wood as the staircase and banister and two columns of the same wood and stained the same. It looked beautiful and like it had always been there.

"Brad I love it. Have you shown it to your Dad yet? I need to talk to him about something. We have set our wedding date for the 29th of December. It will be a small wedding. We will have a BBQ on Saturday for everyone."

"He is at your ranch right now getting ready to put in the foundation for the office tomorrow."

"Sounds great, if he gets the office in the dry before December then I want him to put it on hold and do the wall and French doors."

"I think there is a good possibility it can work. The stable is done now and Cal's house is looking good to be done before Christmas too. He also has a couple more jobs coming to an end soon. I don't think your office and house will be a problem."

"Wonderful, now I am going to take my future bride to Roanoke for dinner. I will talk to you and your Dad later."

"We are going into Roanoke and have a quiet dinner with just the two of us. I told Joyce we wouldn't be home for dinner. I want to spend some time with just us."

"Jackson, I love it. We don't really seem to have much time together."

They drove to the restaurant and sat down to spend the evening together.

They talked about the wedding and how the house was going to look.

"Barbara, I wish it was December right now."

"Darling, I am going to ask Jasper to give me away."

He told her he thought it was a great idea.

"I know he will be thrilled. He loves you like a daughter."

"I'm going to ask Joyce to bake our wedding cake. I would like Jeff to perform the ceremony. What do you think?"

"I think it's perfect, then I can have Cal be my best man."

Jackson thought to himself she really didn't want to go to a lot of trouble for the wedding, but he is going to insist she wear a white wedding dress. It is one thing he is going to insist on. He couldn't wait to see her in it. He knew she would be a beautiful bride. He asked God to help him be the husband she needed.

Chapter Ten

The next morning Marisa came in the office right at 8:30. Barbara asked her if she would like to have a cup of coffee before, they started.

"I would love one. I was afraid I'd be late so I didn't take time this morning. Thank you so much. I am excited about starting this job. I have a feeling we are going to be great friends."

Jackson came in from helping with the chores and asked how they were doing. He gave Barb a sweet kiss and told her to order another desk and anything else they need for Marisa.

"There is a catalog in the office from the office supply company. Use the business credit card and order anything you need and have them deliver it. Order express delivery. You girls have a great day. Sweetheart I will see you at lunch."

"Marisa, we need to get you situated so I can fill you in on what we do. I will be gone from Friday of next week until Sunday night. I would like you to help with the Youth Camp if you don't mind."

"Barbara, I would love to. Where are you going, if I may ask? I don't want to be noisy if you would rather not say."

"It's okay, we have a rodeo on the weekend. Jackson has to deliver some bulls and horses and I will be barrel racing."

"You just let me know what you want me to do. I will come this weekend so you can show me. I love working with children."

They went in the office and Barbara ordered her a computer, desk, a chair and supplies they need for the office. They worked together as she showed her the accounting for the different businesses.

The morning went fast. "Barbara, I sure won't get bored at this job. I love to keep busy."

"Let's go have lunch, I'm sure the guys will be coming in. I will introduce you to everyone."

When they went to the kitchen, they noticed Joyce and Cookie were setting up lunch on the picnic tables outside.

"We thought we would have a little BBQ for our new employee so she can meet everyone. Marisa this is Dalton, but we call him Cookie."

"I'm very happy to meet you Marisa. Welcome to the family. The men are on their way in. Please have a seat and I will get you something to drink."

Barbara looked at Cookie and thought this is the most she ever heard him talk to one person. It was sure interesting. She looked at Joyce and saw her smiling.

The men rode in and went to the bunk house to wash up. When they came out, introductions were made all around.

When Barbara looked over at Marisa, she saw her looking at Chad with a sadness in her eyes. Barbara realized he was probably about the age her son would have been.

"Hi, sweetheart how has your day gone? Marisa are you totally confused yet? When I try to look at all the accounting my head starts to spin. I'm glad I have Barb to take care of it or I would be totally lost."

"This girl is a wonder. You are lucky to have her. I think I will get it all straight soon. She is very thorough in what she does."

Barbara said, "It's not hard, you just have to remember what goes where. Jackson, are you still thinking of adding a clinic for the rodeo riders?"

"I'm still thinking it over. You have so much to take care of now, I hate to over burden you with anything else, especially until after our wedding. By the way folks we are planning a December 29th wedding, so keep the date in mind. We want to start the new year off together."

"The wedding is going to be a small one with our family here on the ranch, Jackson's family and our close friends. We will have a reception the next day for everyone. Jasper would you give me away? Joyce, I want you and Cookie to handle the reception and would you please make my cake for me? We will be getting married here at the house. Don is going to do some remodeling for us before the wedding."

They all said it would be an honor to take care of these things for them.

"Barbara, I will be honored and happy to give you away. You have become like a daughter to me in the short time I have come to know you."

"Thank you for a wonderful lunch and welcoming me to the ranch. I am looking forward to getting to know all of you better."

"Marisa, we are so glad to have you here. If you need anything please feel free to let us know."

"Thank you, Joyce I will. Now I think I best get back to work. Thank you all again."

"Barbara, I can't believe how loving everyone is. I have never worked anywhere before where I felt so welcome. I thank God, he led me to this job."

"God has his hand on this town and the people in it. I felt the same way when I came here."

As the day went on Marisa caught on fast to the job and by the end of the day, she was doing a lot of the work on her own. She had shone Barbara a few accounting tricks she learned over the years and they were working as a team.

The rest of the office furniture arrived and they got Jackson and Chad to help them arrange the office. When they were done, Jackson told them it was time to call it a day.

"Marisa, I am so happy you took this job. You have done a great job today. Have a good evening and I will see you in the morning."

"Jackson, I will let Marisa set up her computer tomorrow. She knows how she wants it. She will have access to all the business accounts. Your personal account, only you and I will have the password for. She is a whiz at accounting. She showed me things I never learned in college."

"Honey, I'm glad you hired her. I think she will make a great addition to our ranch family. Did you see the reaction Cookie and she had to each other? I just love the way this valley works."

"She also had a reaction to Chad when she met him. I have a feeling he is about the age her son would be if he lived."

"I hadn't noticed it at the time, but now you mention it she did seem to get awfully quiet for a minute."

"I noticed Don has the foundation in for the office. He has the pipes run in the concrete so he won't have to put them in the walls. I will talk to him tomorrow when he comes out and see what he thinks his schedule will be."

Joyce came in and told them dinner would be ready in 30 minutes.

Jackson went to check on the bulls and horses. When he came in Joyce was setting dinner on the table. They sat down and grace was said. After dinner Jackson and Barbara went in the den to talk.

"Sweetheart, I love being able to sit here with you enjoying the evening. I will be happy when you don't have to go to the apartment anymore."

"Honey, I love it too. We will be married in a little over three months. I am so glad I hired Marisa. She is really good at what she does. She is interested in working with the children."

"You know I think you are right about her. She seems to fit right in with everyone. "

While they were talking, they heard a car pull up to the house. Jackson went to the door and met Don and his wife as they came on the porch.

"Hi Don and Beth, how are you folks tonight? What can I do for you folks?"

"Jackson, we just came by to talk to you about the work you want done and to tell you how happy we are about your upcoming wedding."

"Please come in, Barbara is in the den. We were just talking about the wedding."

"I have some good news for you then. Your stable is done and I have two other jobs finished. I can get your office and the house done before your wedding. Brad told me you are thinking about having it around Christmas."

"We have set the date for the 29th of December. Barbara, look who dropped by."

"Beth, Don so nice to see you both. Beth, it is so seldom we get to see you other than on Sunday. Would you like a cup of coffee?"

The women went to the kitchen and made coffee while the men talked about the work they wanted done.

"Jackson, I will have a crew in here tomorrow to look at the wall and see what they need to shore it up while they take it out. Once they start, we should be able to have it out and finished in a week. The foundation is already poured for the office. My crew will have the outside walls and roof on in less than a month. Once it is in the dry it won't take long to finish it."

"Don, it sounds great. It will make it a lot easier on Barb and Marisa when they can get into the new office. They are kind of cramped working here in the house."

Barbara and Beth came in with their coffee and the men filled them in on what they were talking about. Barbara said she was happy the work would be done so soon.

"Don, when the office is done, we want the one here in the house turned back into a master suite. We still want the two large windows in the office taken out and patio doors put in."

"I'll have the men do them while they are here working on this wall. It won't take long. It can be done in a day."

"Did Jackson tell you I hired an assistant. She is a member of the United Methodist Church in Roanoke. She is probably pretty close to your and Beth's age. She works with the youth group in her Church."

"Barbara, her name wouldn't happen to be Marisa Moreno, would it?"

"Why yes Beth it is. Do you know her? She came very highly recommended by her last employer and the Church according to Tom."

"I'm sure she did. She is a wonderful person. I have worked with her on several Church committees. It was terrible when she lost her husband and son. They were on their way home from a basketball tournament when her husband lost control of the car on a slick road and went over the side of the mountain. I don't think she is over it."

"Beth, it would be hard enough to lose your husband but to lose a child as well. I don't know how you could really get over it."

"Barbara, Only God can help her through it. I know she has a strong faith. I have seen it in the way she talks about her work with the kids. I think they have helped her through so much."

"She is a great worker and seems to be a wonderful person. I know we are going to be great friends. I hope she will decide to move here instead of driving every day from Roanoke."

"Barbara, I look forward to seeing her again. I will invite her to the Methodist Church here. I know she has been involved with the one in Roanoke for years."

They had their coffee and Barbara told them what she planned for their wedding. "Barbara, if you need any help please let me know."

When they left to go home, Jackson and Barbara went to the den to do their devotions. When they were done, Jackson asked if she would like to go for a walk.

"I would love to; it is a beautiful night. I think we are having our Indian summer."

They walked around the compound hand in hand. Jackson said he would be happy when they could do this as husband and wife. He walked her over to her apartment and gave her a kiss. They said good-night.

Barbara thought how lovely it was to just walk together in the beauty of the night. God was so good. She went up to her apartment and thanked God for such a good man to love, knowing he loved her too.

The next morning Don and his crew showed up to look over the wall and install the French doors in the office.

"Jackson, I have ordered the doors for the family room wall. They will be in tomorrow and we will install them before we take out the wall. We will start on the wall tomorrow. I have put two crews on the office. It won't take long to get it in the dry."

"Thank you, Don we appreciate you doing this so soon. I know you have a lot of work to do. How is the house coming for Cal and Gloria? I know they are anxious to see it done. They want to set a date for their wedding as soon as it's done."

"It's ahead of schedule. We should have it finished before Thanksgiving."

"That is great news. I know Cal will be happy. When it is done, I will have Ellen landscape it for them."

The next morning, when Barbara and Marisa came in, Don told them he was taking out the windows and installing the door this morning. He asked them to cover their computers and printers until they were done so the dust won't get in them.

"That's okay Don, we can work in the den on the lap tops until you get done in here."

"I'll let you know when we are done and have everything cleaned up. If you need anything from here you can come in to get it. We will be working on the wall so the rest of the room will be free."

"Don, can I have Joyce bring you in coffee and donuts?"

"Thank you, but we are fine for right now. Hi Marisa, Beth was glad to hear you were working here with Barbara. I know she plans to come by and see you some time soon. How have you been?"

"Hi Don, I will be happy to see Beth. I always enjoyed working with her at Church. It is so good to see you. I love knowing I have friends living here."

"Don, let Joyce know if you need anything. We will try to not interfere with your work."

Just before noon, Don came in the den and told them they could move back in their office. Everything was done and cleaned up.

"Thank you, Don it will be so good to not have people coming through the house to come in the office."

"Marisa, let's go have lunch before we move back in the office."

Hank and Cal were just coming in for lunch. He asked Barbara if Don has the doors in yet.

"He just finished them. We decided to have lunch before we move back in the office. It will be nice to not have people coming through the house. We need to put a sign up to guide them around to the new entrance."

"I'll see about getting one made for it. How do the doors look?"

"We didn't go in there yet. I'm sure knowing Don's work they are great. We can go look after lunch."

"Well Marisa, how do you like working here? We are glad to have you. Barbara tells me you are a wiz at accounting. Have

145

you thought about moving to Hidden Valley? I know the drive here is long."

"I have been thinking about it. I think I will look and see what is available. It would make it a lot easier not to travel an hour to work."

"Talk to Don, he can help you find a home. He knows the real estate market here. I understand you and Beth are friends."

"Yes, we have worked together at my church in Roanoke. I am looking forward to seeing her again."

After lunch, they all went in to look at the patio doors. They made such a big difference in the look of the room.

"Jackson, I love them. We will need drapes for them when we turn this back into a master suite."

"It looks like the office will be done before we know it. He has really been working on it. He said he has two crews working. It will be great when you can move in. You will have more room. I think you might want to hire a receptionist.

"I think it's something we should think about."

"Jackson, when do we have to leave for North Carolina? My first run is on Friday night."

"I think we will drive there on Thursday evening. You and Red need to rest before your run. I will get rooms at the motel close to the park. They have stalls assigned for the livestock and horses."

"Marisa, will you be alright handling the office on Friday and the girls on the weekend? I hate to overwhelm you so soon."

"Barbara, I will be fine. I am looking forward to working with the girls. I don't know much about barrel racing, but you have a couple of older girls who seem to be good. I'm sure we will be fine."

"I sure am glad God sent you to us. He knew I needed you. We work so well together and you have become family from the first day."

"Everyone here has been so wonderful to me. I have felt like I was home right away. It is a very special place."

"Don and his crew did a great job of cleaning up. You wouldn't know the doors were just put in. He even uncovered our equipment for us."

"I guess it is one reason everyone wants him to build their homes for them."

Don came in and told Jackson his men were moving the furniture in the family room and den around and covering it. They will start tearing out the wall after lunch.

"Thanks Don, have the doors came in yet? I appreciate you doing all of this. I hope we are not getting you behind on any other jobs."

"Everything is fine. We are caught up right now with all the jobs except this one. Cal's house is in the final stages. I have a finishing crew working on it. The doors are to be delivered this afternoon. We will install them tomorrow."

"If it is okay with you, I think we will go out and look at what is done at the office."

"That's fine, it's in the dry and ready for the siding and roofing. We will start on the inside next week. I expect to have it ready for you in about two weeks."

"Don, when we start redoing the master suite down here, I would like to have a jet tub installed. The rooms will need repainting. When we get moved out, we will have a better idea of what needs to be done."

While they were talking, Don heard his men in the family room moving things around.

"Sounds like we are back to work. I guess I'd best go check on my men. Have a good afternoon."

"Well girls, what do you say we go out and look at the office building?"

The three of them walked out to see how much has been done. The crew was starting on the roofing. They waved as they walked up.

When they went in, they saw the rooms were divided and the rest room fixtures were installed. They could get an idea of what it was going to look like.

"Jackson, it is going to be perfect. I think you are right about hiring a receptionist though. It would be inconvenient to run out of our office to talk to people."

"When we get back from the rodeo, place an ad for a receptionist. Whoever you hire can start when we move you in the office."

That evening, when Barbara went to see about dinner, she noticed the wall had been torn down and large 6x6 beams had been placed to hold up the ceiling. Jackson came in as she was looking at it.

"They will come in tomorrow with the beam for the ceiling and the columns. They should have it finished and ready for painting by tomorrow evening. They are going to put in the patio doors tomorrow. It will be ready for our wedding."

"It is going to be beautiful. I can't wait to see it finished. We are going to have a beautiful wedding."

"Darling, I wish our wedding was tomorrow. I love you and can hardly wait to make you my wife. Are you ready for the rodeo? We will be leaving in two days. We will be hauling the horses. George and Davis will be bringing the bulls."

"I'm as ready as I will ever be. I hope I don't disappoint you. It has been a long time since I have ridden in a rodeo. I know Red is ready, I wish I was as sure of myself."

"Sweetheart, I have no doubt you are ready. Just go in there to have fun. Don't worry about winning. You're a winner to me no matter what happens."

They went in to dinner. Jackson said the blessing and Cal told them his house was almost finished. They were going to pick out furniture and window covering this week.

"Cal, I am so happy for you. Have you two picked a wedding date yet? I have spoken to Ellen about your landscaping. All you and Gloria have to do is call her and she will get with you about it."

"Thank you. Jackson, we will get with her. We are planning on getting married in June."

Jackson and Barbara went in to do their devotions and Cal left to meet Gloria at the hospital.

Barbara was up early the next morning and went to the arena to work with Red. She hoped she could make Jackson, and everyone who wanted her to do this again proud.

Jackson came out to feed. He saw her working with Red. She was every bit as good as she was when she was younger. He knew she would do great whether she won or not. He just wanted her to enjoy what she loved doing.

Barbara saw him and waved. "How are you this morning? I thought I would get an early practice in."

"You are looking great. Sweetheart, you have nothing to worry about. You are a winner no matter what happens at the rodeo. You are every bit as good as you were four years ago. Like I told you, we just want you to do what you love doing."

"Jackson, you will never know how much I love you. God has blessed us with a second chance and it is what is important."

When they went to the house, Don and his crew were in the family room working on the dividing columns. He told them his other crew would be there in a few minutes to put in the patio doors. Ellen told him she would be over today to start on the landscaping.

"That is great Don, we will be leaving tomorrow for North Carolina. We will be back late Sunday night. The office is looking good. Thank you so much for all your hard work."

"I have the painters scheduled to come back on Friday to paint the rest of the house. You guys have a good time at the rodeo. I know everything will be great."

When Marisa came in, she and Barbara sat down and went over everything for the weekend at the camp. Barbara told her not to worry about the office. They were caught up on all the accounting and everything else could wait until Monday.

The next morning Jackson, George and Davis loaded the cattle and horses so they could get on the road. Barbara decided to take the pickup and horse trailer for Red. She wasn't sure about trailering him with the rodeo horses.

When Jackson got to the rodeo grounds, he went to find Barbara. He wanted to be sure she made the trip okay and had Red settled in his stall.

When Barbara got to the rodeo grounds, she went to find Red's assigned stall. She was just getting him settled when someone came up to the stall next to her with her horse. Barbara looked up and saw an old friend, she raced barrels with, standing in the stall. "Ramona, how have you been? It is so good to see you."

"Barbara, I can't believe it. Where have you been girl? I have missed competing against you. No one kept me on my toes like you did. It is really good to see you. Are you and Red competing again?"

Jackson walked up to see Barbara and another girl hugging each other and laughing. When he got up close, he saw the other girl was Barbara's old friend from the circuit.

"Ramona hi, how are things going? I'm glad to see you girls found each other."

"Hi Jackson, are you two back together? I never understood what happened between you. You seemed to be so much in love. Barbara where did you disappear to? We were all so worried about you when you just left like you did."

"Ramona, we will set down and talk while we are here. I will explain everything to you. Jackson and I are engaged. We are getting married the 29th of December. Jackson raises rodeo livestock now and I came with him. He talked me into competing again."

"Well I am glad. I have really missed you these last four years. I thought about you every time I came to compete. It is good to have you back. Are you guys staying at the hotel where we always stay? Maybe we can have dinner together tonight and catch up. My husband is here with me and I would like you both to meet him. He has heard me talk about you so often."

"Davis is getting the rodeo stock settled. When he is done, we will get registered at the hotel and meet you and your husband in the dining room at 6:00."

"That sounds great. I'll see you both then. Congratulations on your engagement. I would love to come to your wedding."

They went to check on Davis and the rodeo livestock. Jackson asked her if she was glad, she came now. She told him she was so glad to see Ramona. She is glad to know she is still a friend. She was afraid everyone would resent her for leaving like she did.

They went to register at the hotel and meet Ramona and her husband for dinner. When they entered the dining room, Jackson noticed one of his rodeo buddies setting with Ramona. "Rand, how are you doing? So, you are Ramona's husband. It is great to see you."

"Jackson, good to see you. Ramona just told me you and Barbara are engaged. Congratulations, I wondered where you had gone when you left the rodeo."

"I have a ranch in Virginia. I raise rodeo livestock and run a Youth Ranch. I bought out the Bar-Nun Livestock and Jasper's rodeo contracts. I would like to talk to you about something while we are here."

"Well no time like the present. I would love to see your ranch and learn more about the Youth Ranch."

"I have been thinking about opening the ranch, to anyone who would like to spend time during the rodeo off season, as a camp to hone their skills. They would spend six-weeks at the ranch. They would have a bunk house to live in and meals as well as the best bulls and broncs to work with. Do you think it will be something most of the riders would be interested in?"

"I know it is something I would be interested in. I'm sure there are a lot of others who will be. Will you also be opening it to the barrel racers? I couldn't be gone long from Ramona."

"We will be offering it to the barrel racers and married couples will have a room in the main house. The next rodeo is at Harrisonburg. Why don't you and Ramona come to Hidden Valley and spend some time at the ranch after the rodeo?

We are only 45 miles from Roanoke. We have plenty of room and would love to have you."

"That sounds like a great idea. We would love to come and see your ranch and check out the Youth Ranch."

When they finished eating, they went to the rodeo grounds to check on the horses. Then they went back to the hotel and Jackson walked Barbara to her room, he gave her a kiss and told her he would meet her in the morning for breakfast.

Chapter Eleven

When they went down to breakfast, they saw Rand and Ramona sitting at a table with a couple of the bull riders. When they walked over, the men all greeted each other and they sat down to eat. Jackson knew the other men and they started talking about the camp, Rand and Jackson discussed the night before. They told Jackson they would be interested in the camp when he decided to open it.

Jackson told them, "I will get in touch with you when I have made arrangements to start. I have to build two more bunk houses before I can begin."

When they got to the rodeo grounds the girls went to get their horses ready for the barrel racing.

"Barbara, I am going to check on the livestock and will be back to watch you ride."

He gave her a kiss and told her to just have fun.

They ran the barrels five times during the rodeo from Friday night to Sunday night.

Barbara won three of the runs and Ramona won two. They were so close for all their runs. They were both happy with the outcome.

Ramona told her she was so glad she was back.

Jackson's livestock scored well for all the events. He was happy with the outcome. He knew he had some good livestock.

Sunday night they all said good-bye. Ramona told Barbara she would see her next week at Harrisonville. They were looking forward to seeing the ranch the next week.

"Jackson, are you planning on bringing livestock to the rodeo at Harrisonville? I thought you have to preach next Sunday."

"Honey, I do. Davis and George are taking the livestock. I want you to go. I think you should take Marisa and the girls with you. The older girls can compete. It will give them some experience. I will pay their fees. Marisa can be with the two younger ones while you compete. You can take the Motor Home and pull the four- horse trailer."

"Jackson, I don't know about pulling the four-horse trailer with the motor home. It is so big. I'm not comfortable doing it."

"Honey, I will drive you up on Friday morning. Marisa can follow us in my car. I will drive it back home and come back after Church on Sunday to watch all of you compete and drive you home."

"It is a lot of traveling for you. If you don't mind and Marisa is willing then I guess it will work."

"Darling, everything will work out fine. I want to be there Sunday night to see you all compete and be with you. I am so glad you are doing what you love again."

"I will miss you. I do love competing again though. I didn't realize how much I have missed it until this weekend."

"Barb, Davis and George are going to haul the livestock back to the ranch. I am going to ride with you. I'm going to help them load the livestock and will be back here in about an hour."

Barbara went in to get Red ready to load in the horse trailer.

"Ramona, I will see you next Friday at Harrisonville. I am bringing the girls from the Youth Camp. Jackson is going to pay the fee for the two older ones to complete. You will like them. They love the sport and are getting really good at it."

"Barb, I am so glad to see you riding again. I have really missed you. When we come to your ranch next week we will sit down and have a talk."

When Jackson got back to the stable, Barb had the trailer hooked up and was loading Red. They said good-bye to Ramona and Rand. They would see them next week.

On the way home, they talked about the Rodeo Camp and what they would need to do in order to get it established.

"Jackson, you need to figure out the expense of running it in order to determine what you will have to charge. We will sit down when we get home and work on an expense chart."

"Sweetheart, I will let you take care of it. I have no idea when it comes to finances. I am so blessed to have you. I would probably be in the hole in a year if I was trying to figure it out."

"We will sit down and make a list of what the cost would be and see where we will need to go from there. You need to call Don and Brad when you get home and get a cost for the bunk houses, then we will figure out what it will cost to feed them for six weeks, cost of the electric as well as the feed for the horses. I have your personal finances done for you. You need to take it to Tom. Have him check your investments and see if they need to be changed to get you a better return."

"I will give him a call and we will make an appointment to talk with him."

It was late when they pulled up to the stable. They unloaded Red and bedded him down for the night. Jackson told Barbara he was going to the house and make coffee. He needed to stay up until Davis and George got there with the livestock. He would need to help unload them and put them up for the night.

While they were walking up to Barbara's apartment, they saw the trucks and trailers coming down the lane. He told her good night and went to help with the livestock. She asked him if he would like her to make coffee for them.

"I don't think they will want any. We will probably all be ready for bed when we get them taken care of. I will see you in the morning. I love you so much."

He kissed her and left to go help the men.

When Barbara came in the kitchen the next morning, Joyce asked her how she did at the rodeo.

"I got three first and two second place wins. I am pleased with it all. I didn't expect to do so well after being out of the circuit for so long."

When Jackson and Cal came in for breakfast, Cal said, "the office is done and we moved the office furniture. It really is a nice place. You girls will have plenty of room now. You need to get a receptionist soon though."

"Thank you, Cal. I will call an ad in this morning for the receptionist. I appreciate you guys moving everything for us. Are the computers hooked up yet?"

"Everything is up and running for you. I think you will really like it when you see it."

"Cal, I talked to some of the guys at the rodeo and they are interested in the camp we talked about. A couple, who are friends of Barb and mine, will be here after the rodeo next weekend. They will be staying a few days. Joyce will you please get one of the bedrooms ready for them? They are a married couple."

When Marisa came in, they went out to the office to look everything over. It really looked nice and gave them so much more room. Barbara went to her office and put a call in for a receptionist.

"Marisa, what would you think about going to the rodeo with me and the girls next weekend. It is in Harrisonville? Jackson will drive the motor home there for us to stay in. I will need you and a couple of the girls to drive his SUV there so he will have a way back. He is preaching at the Spanish Church next Sunday so he won't be able to stay for the rodeo."

"I would love to. Are any of the girls riding? I would love to go see you ride."

"I want the two older girls to ride if they will. Jackson will pay their fee. I think they will love it and it will give them some experience."

Cal came in to see if everything was where they wanted it. "Cal, it is great. You did a wonderful job of putting it all where it needed to be."

"Cal is your house done yet? I know you were going to look at furniture when we left."

"It is all done and the furniture arrived yesterday. You and Jackson need to come out and see it after dinner. We are arranging everything where we want it now."

"I would love to. I know it is beautiful. I bet Gloria is excited. I know I would be if I were her."

"We are thinking about moving our wedding up, now the house is done. We are waiting to hear from her parents to see when they would be able to come. Her son has been living with them while she is getting established here and in her job. I am anxious to get to know him. He is three years old. She has really missed him the last few months."

"I didn't realize she has a son. I know you will love him. I know how you Barnes men are about children. I bet she is anxious to get her life together for her and her son. When are you thinking about getting married?"

"We are thinking about sometime around the first week of December."

"I don't know how much landscaping you will have done for it but knowing Ellen she will figure something out to make it beautiful for the wedding."

"Barb, I need your advice about something. I want one of my brothers to perform the ceremony and the other to be my best man, but I don't know how to choose."

"Well Cal, Jeff is officiating at our wedding, so I don't think it will make a difference, if you want Jackson to be the pastor for your wedding. Talk it over with him. I'm sure he really won't care. He'll just be happy for you."

"Thank you, and I will talk to him tonight. Gloria has a call in to her parents. She will probably hear from them today."

"You know you can have your wedding here at the house. It is a beautiful place for it now. Opening up those rooms made such a difference."

"We have talked about it. Would you mind if we have our wedding here before yours?"

"Of course not. We are all family. I'm just happy for you both."

Jackson came in and told them it was quitting time. Joyce said lunch was ready.

"How do you lady's like your new office space? It sure gives you a lot more room to work."

"We love it. I called in the ad for a receptionist. Hopefully it won't take long to hire one. I need to order a computer and office chair for her. She will only be setting appointments on the computer. I don't want anyone doing the accounting and bookkeeping but Marisa and I."

When they sat down for lunch, Cal told Jackson he would like to talk to him about something.

"Well Bother what is it you need? You know I will do anything for you."

"Gloria and I have decided since the house's done, we will get married the first part of December instead of waiting till summer. We were wanting to have the wedding here if it is alright with you and Barb. Barb said it is fine with her. I also wanted either you or Jeff to officiate at the ceremony and the other one to be my best man."

"Cal, it would be great if you have the wedding here. I would love to officiate at the wedding. It would be an honor. Talk to Jeff and see if it will be alright with him. He can be your best man if he agrees. It is late to do a lot of landscaping at your house. I know Ellen has started putting in some trees and bushes, but the flowers will have to wait."

"Gloria is waiting to hear from her parents before we set a date. Thank you, she will be thrilled to know we can have the ceremony here."

Jackson went in the office to talk to Barb after lunch.

"Honey, are you sure it is okay with you for Cal and Gloria to have their wedding here before we have ours?"

"Jackson, I told Cal it was fine. I mentioned it to him before he said anything. I am glad they are going to get married sooner. They need to do it now and get moved into their new home. Did you know Gloria has a three-year old son? They need to be a family now."

"No, I didn't, Cal never said anything to me about it. Where is the boy now?"

"He said her parents have him since she moved here, so she could get settled in her job. She is anxious to get him home with her."

"It will be nice to have another nephew to spoil. I know she will be glad to get the wedding over and get them all settled in their new home."

Barbara called the girl's parents to get permission to take them to Harrisonville for the rodeo. They were all in agreement. Some of them said they would come to the rodeo to watch them compete.

Barbara got a call from an applicant for the receptionist job as she was closing the office. She made an appointment for her to come in for an interview in the morning.

They closed the office and Barb asked Marisa if she has found a home to rent in the Valley yet.

"Barbara, I have an appointment this evening to look at one which sounds promising. Don and Beth told me about it. The lady who owns it is moving to Florida to be with her daughter and her family."

"I'll be praying it is what you need. I don't like you traveling so far to work. With winter coming on it is too dangerous."

"Thank you. I have a good feeling about this home. Don says it is in good shape. I think she would like to sell it. I would love to buy one here. I won't have any trouble selling my home in Roanoke. I already have someone who would love to buy it."

Barbara told her, "We will be praying for everything to work out and real soon. It will be wonderful to have you living close."

Marisa left to go look at the house. She thought how special it was to have a friend like Barbara and to work with her.

"Jackson, Marisa Is going to look at a house. She may buy it. I hope she will. I like the idea of having her living close. I have become very fond of her."

Cal came in for dinner and said "Gloria heard from her folks and they have set the wedding for December 2nd. It will be on a Saturday."

"Barbara, Gloria asked me to find out if you would be her maid-of-honor."

"Cal, tell her I will be honored to. I will get with her to help plan the wedding. We have a lot to do between now and then."

"I talked to Jeff and he is fine with you officiating at the wedding and him being my best-man. Gloria's parents will be here next week. I will be moving in the house this weekend and they will stay with me when they get here."

"You can bring them here for meals. Especially when Gloria is working. I know what a great cook you are."

"Don't get smart brother. I am a better cook than you. At least I can boil water."

"Cal, what shift is Gloria working this week? Is she off any during the week? I will be gone all weekend to the rodeo. I would like to talk to her about the wedding before then if possible."

"She is on days this week. I will have her come out for dinner tomorrow night."

Cal left to go meet Gloria at the new house. They wanted to be sure everything will be ready for him to move in and to get a room ready for her parent's and son. She was having Les Jones come and paint the little one's room for him with animals on the wall.

"Jackson, I will have to get with Ellen about flowers for the house and some plants that we can keep. It will be fun getting it ready for them and I can see what I will want for our wedding. They will only be a few weeks apart."

"Honey, you are going to have your hands full with work the wedding and the rodeos. Please don't wear yourself out. Get help with what you need. We will have someone come in to clean the house. I will let Joyce know she can hire a caterer for the wedding and rehearsal dinner."

Barbara couldn't wait to talk to Gloria about the wedding. She always wanted a sister to do these things with. She would have to be careful to not try to take it over.

"Jackson, let's take a ride out to the house and see it. Cal has gone out there to meet Gloria."

"Let's saddle the horses and ride out. We have time before it gets dark."

When they got to the house it looked beautiful up against the mountain and trees. Barbara told Jackson she loved it. They tied their horses and went in. Gloria was happy to see them. She gave them a hug and told them to come look it over.

"Barbara, thank you for agreeing to be my maid-of-honor. I can't thank you enough for letting us get married in your home. I know you wanted to get married there first. Are you sure it is alright with you?"

"Gloria, I offered before Cal mentioned it. It is fine with me. We are family now. When your mother gets here, we will start planning the wedding. Jackson is hiring a caterer for the wedding dinner and the rehearsal dinner. We can get with Ellen about the flowers for the house."

"I know there is a lot to do and not much time to do it in. I appreciate all you and Jackson are doing. I have always wanted a sister and now I have a bunch."

"You are not alone. I am an only child too. We sure are inheriting a great bunch of siblings."

"Barb, we need to head back to the house. It will be getting dark soon and we rode the horses here."

On the way back, Jackson said he was happy for his brother. They really seemed to be happy. He wished their wedding was as soon as Cal and Gloria's. Barb told him they were only a few weeks apart.

"Honey, I know but I can't help wishing it was sooner. I love you and can't wait to be with you always."

"I know and it will be here sooner than you think. We have a lot to do before we can go on a honeymoon. I love you more than you can imagine."

When they got back to the stable, they took care of their horses and went out to look at where they wanted to build the new bunk houses.

"Jackson, have you ever thought about holding rodeos here? You have the ideal place for it. If you decided to, I could apply for certification with the National Rodeo Association for you."

"You know, I have never thought about it but you are right. We have both the inside arena which is large enough as well as the room for an outside arena. We would have to build bleachers for the outside arena."

"If you did decide to do it, would you keep hauling livestock to the other rodeo's or just use them here?"

"If we got certified to have rodeos here then I would probably just use my livestock here. Do me a favor and see what you can find out about getting certified. I like the idea of being able to have our own rodeo here."

"I will do some checking, and you can talk it over with Cal. Maybe Jasper can give you some ideas as well."

They went in the house and got a cup of coffee. Then they went in the den to do their devotions, before it was time for Barbara to go to her apartment.

After their devotions, Jackson walked her to her apartment and gave her a sweet kiss and told her he loved her. He left and went back to the house thinking about how soon they wouldn't have to be apart. He thanked God for all he has done in his and Cal's lives. He has given them the perfect mates to live their lives with. He was happy for his brother, but he kind of wished it was him getting married on the 2nd of December instead of the 29th.

Barbara went to bed thinking about how happy she was for Gloria and wishing her wedding was sooner. They have so many things going on right now. She liked the idea of having the rodeos here though. Then they wouldn't be doing as much traveling. She really didn't need to attend so many rodeos. She wasn't interested in trying for the nationals. She would be happy just riding when they had one here.

The next morning, Barbara went to the house early. She wanted to look up the requirements for the National Rodeo Association. She asked God to guide them in whatever they decide to do. When she went in the kitchen, Jackson was there having coffee. He gave her a kiss and asked her what she was doing up so early.

She told him what she was planning on doing. She thought she would get the information and then he and Cal could talk about it.

"Honey, do we want to add something else to our schedule before the wedding? I love the idea and would like to see if we can do it. I don't want anything to interfere with us getting married when we plan."

"Sweetheart, we will not let anything interfere with us getting married. We will leave it in God's hands. If this is what we are meant to do then things will come together, if not then he is telling us to wait. We don't have to do anything right away. I just wanted to find out what we will need to do when the time comes. It will give you and Cal a chance to see if it is something you would even want to pursue."

"I really do like the idea. See what you can find out. It will give us time to decide if it is feasible for the ranch. I don't want anything to interfere with the Youth Ranch though."

When she checked on the requirements for the rodeo, she knew they had the required acreage for it. She started a chart to see how they could lay it out and where they would have to place the bunk houses, they planned to build so they wouldn't interfere with it. There would be a lot of things to be considered. They would need to talk about setting up a future plan so they wouldn't have anything in the way of working it out.

Jackson came in to see what she found out. She showed him the requirements. He looked it over and told her they would have to reconsider where the bunk houses would go if they were going to consider doing it.

"Honey come in for breakfast. We will go over all of this later when Cal can be here with us."

They went back to the house to have breakfast. Cal was sitting at the table. Jackson asked him what he had going this morning.

"If you have time, I would like you to come over to the office after breakfast to talk about something."

"I can take the time to talk. The men are out checking the fences. What is up?"

"Barb and I have been talking about something I need your opinion about, as it effects the ranch."

"Okay, let's go to the office after we get done eating. As long as it doesn't interfere with either of our weddings, I am all for it."

"How do you know before you even hear what I have to say?"

"Because anything the two of you come up with will only help the ranch. You both tend to know what the other needs and what the ranch needs."

After breakfast they all went out to the office. Marisa had just arrived and had coffee on. She offered them a cup and asked Barbara if there was anything she needed before she started on her work. Barbara told her they would be in her office discussing some business.

"Marisa, the women who applied for the receptionist job will be here in an hour. Go ahead and interview her. If you like her call me and I will come out and speak to her."

Jackson, Cal and Barbara went in her office. Jackson told Cal what they talked about. Barbara showed them the information she pulled up showing the requirements for the ranch to hold an NRA approved rodeo. They looked over the chart Barbara prepared, showing where they would need to put the outside arena. They would have to place the bunk houses in a different location to make it work.

"Jackson, would you still be hauling livestock to other rodeos? If you held more than one here it would put a lot on you and Davis to keep ahead."

"I am thinking if this works out, I will use the livestock here and not make any new contracts with other rodeos. I will have to fulfill the ones I have though."

"I like the idea of you being here more. I think we should check into it. With the black angus we are raising, the Rodeo Camp and the Youth Camp, if we held three rodeos a year, we would have the ranch in good shape."

"Okay, I will see about applying with the National Rodeo Association and see how things go. We can start with the next Rodeo season. That will give you guys time to get everything ready after both of our weddings. Now you two go to work, Marisa and I have work to do."

Chapter Twelve

Marisa called Barbara and told her the lady was there for her interview.

"Marisa, I'll be right out. Take her to your office and I will meet you there."

When she went in Marisa's office, she realized she knew the lady sitting there, from Church. They greeted each other and Barbara introduced her to Marisa as Shirley Mason. She also has a son attending the Youth Camp. She said they know each other from church.

They talked a while and Marisa explained to her what her job would entail. Barbara told her what her pay would be and after 60 days she would have benefits, the company would pay for.

Shirley said it sounded good to her. They welcomed her to the family. Marisa gave her the employment papers to fill out and explained a background check would be done because of the Youth Camp.

"That will be fine. I look forward to working with you. I will be here in the morning and thank you for this opportunity."

"Barb, I think she will fit right in. She seems like a really nice person and has the right kind of personality for the job."

"I don't know her well, but I have always liked her. Her son seems like a very nice young man. They are both a little quiet at times. I think maybe they have not had an easy life."

Barbara sent for the paper work to learn what they needed to do, in order to get the ranch certified for the National Rodeo circuit. She pulled up what she could on the internet so they could be looking it over before the actual papers came. She told Marisa she was going out to the stable to talk to Jackson and would be back in a little while.

"Marisa, if you need me, call my cell phone. We will be out by the stable."

When she got out to the stable, she saw Jackson working with the filly he bought when he bought Red. She was a beautiful horse. She looked a lot like her shire.

Jackson saw Barbara standing in the entrance to the arena. He smiled at her and walked over to see what she needed.

"Hi there, what did I do to get the honor of seeing you in the middle of the day again. Isn't she a beauty? She is going to be a great addition to the ranch. I have been calling her Beauty. Jasper said he never got around to naming and registering her. We need to get it done."

"I think Beauty is a good name for her. We can register her as Big Red's Beauty."

"It sounds good to me. You need to go ahead and send in her registration papers. She is already 10 months old. What did you need Honey? I know you didn't just come out to just see me."

"Shirley Mason from Church is the person, who came in for the receptionist job. She will start tomorrow. Do you want me to have Tom do a background check, even though we know her? I also wanted us to go look at where the outside arena needs to be placed. We need to decide where we will need to put the bunk houses. I have sent for the paper work to see what will be required, in order to have a rodeo here."

"I will ask Tom if we need a background check on Shirley. She won't be working with the kids and her son attends the camp.

Let me put Beauty away. We will go walk around and see where we think the outside arena should be. When we get the information on the size it has to be, we will have a better idea where to put the bunk houses.

We will also have to put in restrooms for people who come to watch the rodeo."

While they were walking around looking at the area Cal and Davis came up. Jackson filled Davis in on what they were thinking about doing. He told them he loved the idea.

"Jackson, I think it will work out great. You can also have junior rodeos for the youth. It will bring a lot of people and also show what the Youth Camp is doing. The advertising for the Youth Camp will be great. You really have the ideal set up for all of it."

They decided the outdoor arena should be in an area close to the indoor arena. The decided they could have the restrooms put between the two. They would be convenient and separate the two areas. They decided to build the two-new bunk houses close to the others.

"Jackson, I think we will probably eventually need to build a kitchen and dining room in order to have room for everyone when we get more people here."

"You know Cal I think you are probably right. We are going to have to start thinking about the cost of all the construction and how long it will take to recoup our money."

"I will start working on a budget when I get the papers from National and see what we will have to pay to get certified. Then we can talk to Brad and Don about the cost of the buildings and bleachers for the outdoor arena. I need to get back to work now. I will see you at dinner."

When Barbara got back to the office, Marisa said a buyer called to talk to Jackson about the Black Angus cattle. She told him she would have her or Jackson give him a call.

Barbara called Jackson and told him about the call. He said he would be over to the office in a few minutes. When Jackson got to the office, he went to Barbara's office to place the call. The buyer was interested in looking over the cattle for his chain of restaurants. Jackson told him to come out the next morning and he would take him around and talk.

"Barb, I think when this buyer gets the ones' he wants we will put the cattle back in the pasture we brought them in from. I want them to have plenty of grass to graze on. I don't want to have to feed them and not be able to sell them as grass fed."

"Will you need to have the men help you drive them back out there? I'm sure it is the right thing to do."

"I'm sure we can drive them back with our own men. We can probably do it in one day. I will take Cookie with us. He can help with the cattle and we will cook over a camp fire. Once we get them away from the compound, they will take care of themselves. We won't have to go as far with them this time. I will send some of the men out to check on them every couple of weeks. I can't sell them as free-range cattle if I keep them penned"

"Do you want me to make copies of their breeding for this new buyer? When is he coming out to look them over?"

"Honey, it would great if you would make copies for him. He will be here in the morning, probably around nine."

Jackson left to go back out and talk to Cal about the buyer and moving the cattle this week out to the open range.

"Barbara, I bought the house I told you about. I am moving into it this weekend. She just painted and cleaned it so I don't have to do anything but move in. It is a beautiful little bungalow style home. It has three bedrooms and two baths. It is only about three miles from here. I am looking forward to getting moved."

"Marisa, Jackson, Cal and I will be happy to help you move. If you have large furniture to move, we will bring a couple of trucks. We will talk to Jackson after work."

"Barb, it would be wonderful if you would. She is leaving the living room furniture, but I need to bring my dining room furniture and my bed room furniture."

When they closed the office, they went out to talk to Jackson and Cal. They told her they would be happy to help her.

"Marisa, is the house empty now, where you can move in during the week. We can move you one evening. The rodeo is this weekend, so if you can move during the week it would be great."

"Oh, I forgot about the rodeo. Yes, she moved out and left for Florida to be with her daughter and her family. I can move in anytime."

"We will get a couple of the men to help and we can get you moved tomorrow night after work. Will it work for you?"

"Yes, I will pack everything tonight I want to bring. I will sell my house after I get everything taken care of. If we can get the furniture moved, I can take care of the rest next week when we get back from the rodeo. You don't know how much I appreciate your help."

"It is no problem; you are part of the family. We owe you more than this for all the work you do."

Marisa left for home thinking she does have a family again. It felt so good to know they considered her a part of their family.

After dinner, Jackson and Barbara went in the den to do their devotions and talk. Barbara told him she pulled up the requirements for the size of the indoor and outdoor arenas. She told him the indoor arena was the perfect size. She gave him the size of the outdoor arena so they could measure it off and see how everything will fit.

"Honey, I will get with Cal tomorrow and we will measure off the area. Then we will know where to put all the other buildings. We need to talk to Brad and Don and get some estimates on the work needing to be done. Jasper called and said he has his ranch sold and will be arriving here this weekend. He said he would like to come Sunday to see you and the girls ride."

"Jackson, I am so glad he got it sold and will be moving here. I hope he knows he is welcome to live here as long as he wants. He is like the father I always wished I'd had."

"I've told him to take his time finding a place to live. He is special to both of us. I told him about our plans to get certified to hold rodeos here and he said he would like to invest in it. What do you think about taking investors in the rodeo?"

"I think it might work as long as you are careful about who you let invest. I think it will be a good investment for Jasper because of his love of the rodeo."

They finished their devotions and asked God to bless the work they are planning, and to help them make sure it glorified him.

Jackson walked Barbara to her apartment and told her he wished their wedding would hurry up and get there. He gave her a gentle kiss and told her goodnight.

Barbara went to bed thinking how much she loved him and wished their wedding was sooner too. She got to thinking, why couldn't they get married sooner. The house would be decorated for Cal and Gloria's wedding. What if they have their wedding the next week? It would save a lot of work not having to get the house ready twice. Maybe she will talk to Jackson about it. They were planning a small wedding so there wouldn't be many people to contact and they haven't sent out announcements. They could just announce it in Church like Cal and Gloria are doing. The more she thought about it the more she liked the idea. She would talk to Jackson tomorrow. She went to sleep with a smile on her face.

Barbara went to breakfast the next morning excited about talking to Jackson. Jackson was just getting a cup of coffee when she entered the kitchen. She smiled at him and told him she wanted to talk to him about something.

"Good morning darling, you look like you had a good night's sleep. What is it you want to talk to me about?"

"Jackson, what would you think about us moving our wedding up to the weekend after Cal and Gloria's? The house would already be decorated and it would save a lot of work for everyone. We could postpone our honeymoon until after they get back from theirs. I really don't want to wait any longer to get married to you. What do you think?"

"Honey, if you are sure this is what you want to do, I am all for it. We could get married tomorrow and I would be happy."

Cal came in for breakfast while they were talking. Jackson told him they have some news for him.

"Cal, would you be willing to postpone your honeymoon for a week? I want you to be my best-man and Barbara and I have decided to move our wedding up to the weekend after your and Gloria's."

"Jackson, I will talk to Gloria about it, but I don't think she will mind. What about the ranch, if we are both gone on our honeymoons at the same time?"

"We will wait until you get back from yours before we go on ours. Talk it over with Gloria."

Joyce had been listening to them discuss the weddings. She was glad they were moving their wedding up. She will be happy to bake two wedding cakes instead of one. She smiled at them and told them she thought it was a great idea.

They all sat down to breakfast and Jackson said grace. He thanked God for all the blessings He has given them.

The buyer, Marc Wade, showed up to look at the cattle right at nine. He liked the looks of the cattle and tagged what he wanted. He told Jackson he would buy from him from now on.

"You have a great looking bunch of cattle here and I like the idea of them being free range. When can you deliver them to Roanoke? I'll make arrangements at the processing plant for them."

"We can deliver them tomorrow morning, if it will work for them. We are moving the rest out to the open range this week."

"I will give them a call and tell them to expect them tomorrow then. It is great doing business with you. I hear you run a Youth Ranch here as well as the cattle."

"Yes, we have the Youth Ranch as well as rodeo livestock. We are looking at holding rodeos here as soon as we can get certified with the National Rodeo Association."

"That would be great. I know for sure me and my family will be here for the rodeos. Let me know if you ever need any investors.

My father rode broncs when he was younger. He said he remembered you from when you rode."

"Who is your father? Did he ride at the same time I did? There were a great many good riders before my time?"

"He retired the year you won your first National Championship. He said he knew you were going to be a great rider the first time he saw you ride. His name was Marshall Wade."

"I remember Marshall, he was a great rider in his time. I think he won as many championships as I did. Tell him hello for me and to stop out sometime. I would love to see him and talk about the rodeo."

"I will, and maybe I will come with him. I would love to hear more about your plans here."

"You are more than welcome anytime. Let's go over to the office and we can settle up and make arrangements to deliver the cattle."

When they entered the office, Jackson took Marc to Barbara's office. He introduced them and Marc wrote a check for the cattle. Jackson told Barbara about Marc's father and she told them she had met his father at the rodeo when she was 16 years old. He came over to tell her she would be a champion barrel racer someday.

"I don't think dad has ever missed a rodeo within 100 miles of here since he retired. It is why I know he would love to come out and see what you have planned here. You have a great place here. If you ever decide to put a restaurant here, when you get the rodeo going, I would love the opportunity to do it."

"We have talked about needing to put in a kitchen and dining room before we get the rodeo going. I am also opening up a camp for the rodeo riders to come during the off season to work on their skills."

"I will call you when dad can come out and talk to you. Maybe we can talk some more about the rodeo then. Think about the idea of putting in a restaurant. I would be willing to lease a place for it and have it built. It would not be an expense for you and would give you more revenue for the ranch."

"I will talk it over with my bother and Barbara and we will talk again."

Marc left and Jackson called Cal and asked him to come over to Barb's office for a minute. He said he would be right over.

"What is going on? I see the buyer tagged some cattle. When do we need to deliver them and where?"

"They go to Roanoke tomorrow, but it is not what I need to talk to you about. It seems like this rodeo idea is growing fast. If we get the certification, then the buyer who was just here would like to lease a place to build a restaurant here. His father is one of the older rodeo riders. I told him you, Barbara and I would talk it over. Barbara will need to be involved in order for us to keep the financial part of all of this together."

"I think it might be a good idea, but we need to find out if we can even get the permits to have the rodeos here. I'm glad you realize we need Barbara to keep the financial part of it feasible. I know you brother; you get an idea and go after it before you think everything through."

"That is why I made you my partner and have Barb as my accountant. Between the two of you I get a reality check every once in a while. So, what do the two of you think?

"Well Brother, I think it is a sound idea if he is financing the restaurant himself. It is a win for us."

"I agree with Cal, but we need to hear from the NRA first before we make too many plans. It would also mean we will have to figure out where a restaurant would need to be placed. We have a lot of building going on. We also have to apply for all the permits before we can build anything."

Marisa came in the office with an express envelope from the NRA. She gave it to Barbara and told them she hoped it is good news.

Barbara opened it and read the letter and looked at the paper work in the envelope.

"Well, the Association is happy we want to apply for certification as an NRA event. They look forward to looking over our application. They will be sending someone from the association to talk to us as soon as they receive the paperwork. I will fill these out today and send them back express mail so we will know what we need to do next."

"Honey, that is great. It looks like we will know soon enough if this is what we want to do."

"Hey, I wanted to let you know I talked to Gloria and she is fine with us postponing our honeymoon so you two can get married the next weekend. It looks like we are all going to be busy for the next few weeks. I will go arrange for Davis and Chad to deliver the cattle to Roanoke. See you guys at dinner."

"Well sweetheart, it looks like we will be married in about three weeks. We need to invite everyone over tomorrow night so we can tell them our plans. I will call Tom, Hank and Jeff if you will call Meredith and Beth. I will tell Hank to have Anna tell her family to come. Now I need to go tell Joyce we are having a family dinner tomorrow night."

The men left and Barbara started filling out the paper work for the NRA.

"Marisa, let me know if you need me for anything. I will be busy filling out this paper work."

"We are caught up with the accounting so just do what you need to do and I will take care of any calls for you. Shirley is being a great help with making copies and handling calls."

"I am sure things will go smoothly here with the three of us. It is nice to be able to work with people who truly like each other. It is wonderful to know we are all Christians. We will get your furniture moved right after work. We want you to come here for dinner."

Barbara got the papers filled out and mailed back to the rodeo association. She told Marisa it was time to get the men and go pick up her furniture. When they got over to the house Jackson and Cal were waiting for them along with George and Davis.

"You girls ready to go after Marisa's furniture? Joyce will have dinner ready for us when we get back. Marisa, you are staying to eat with us when we get done. We would love for you to spend the night here and get your house ready tomorrow to stay there."

"Jackson, I appreciate the offer and I would love to stay for dinner, but I want to stay in my new home tonight."

"It is up to you. Leave your car here and you and Barbara can take the SUV. It will haul more than your little car."

Barbara and Marisa left in the SUV and the men followed in two trucks. They drove the large trucks so they could carry more furniture in a load.

When they got to Marisa's home in Roanoke the men got busy loading the dining room furniture in one of the trucks. Barbara and Marisa loaded everything she had packed the night before in the SUV. When they got done the men had the bed room furniture loaded. They left to go back to Hidden Valley.

"Barb, we will go to the house and eat before we unload the furniture at Marisa's. Joyce called and said it would be ready by the time we get there."

"Marisa, Jackson said dinner will be ready when we get to the house. We will eat and then go unload everything."

"That is fine, I am getting a little hungry myself. Thank you so much for doing this for me. You and Jackson have been so good to me since I came to work for you."

"Marisa, you are a part of our family now. We love you and want to help you anyway we can."

When they got to the house, Joyce had diner on the table for them. After they ate, they went to Marisa's new home. Barbara told her she loved it. It looked just like what Marisa would be comfortable in.

Marisa had driven her car to the house, so when everything was unloaded, they left to let her get her bed made so she could rest. Barbara told her to take it easy and not to worry about coming in to work tomorrow.

"Stay home and get your house straightened out. There is nothing pressing right now. I'll call you if something comes up. Just take your time and don't overdo."

She thanked everyone for their help. She appreciated everything they have done for her.

They left to go home and have their devotions and spend time together.

"Barb, everyone will be out tomorrow night for diner. We need a lot of help getting everything done for two weddings. Let me know what you will need me to do. I can't believe we are really going to get married sooner. I love you so much. I know God is blessing us with everything going on in our lives. I have a good feeling about everything happening."

"Everyone will pitch in; don't you remember all the help everyone gave to Bill and Rhonda when they changed their wedding date. The valley has a lot of wonderful people here."

When Barbara entered the office the next morning, Shirley told her she had a call from the National Rodeo Association. They left a telephone number for her to call.

Barbara went in her office and placed a call to the rodeo association. When she got off the phone, she called Jackson and asked him and Cal to come to her office when they could.

"We will be there in about 30 minutes. What is happening? I hope it is not bad news."

"No honey, it is actually good news. I will fill you both in when you get here."

"Cal meet me in Barbara's office as soon as you get done here. She said she needs to talk to the two of us. I am going over there right now."

"Okay, I will be there in a about 15 minutes. Do you know what she needs to talk to us about?"

"She said she would tell us when we get there. She said it is good news though."

Jackson headed over to the office. He was wondering what could be so important she needed to talk to them both.

"Hi Shirley, how are you liking your job. I hope everything is going good for you here."

"Hi Jackson, everything is great. I love working for Barbara and with Marisa. They are both great ladies and have made me feel so welcome. She is in her office. She said to tell you and Cal to go right in."

"Cal will be here in a few minutes. Send him in when he gets here."

Jackson went to Barbara's office. He was anxious to find out what was happening.

"Hi sweetheart, what is going on. Cal will be here in a few minutes. I love seeing you again, but we just had breakfast together. What happened between then and now?"

"We had a call from the rodeo association. I need to fill you and Cal in on the conversation. They are sending a representative out in the morning to look things over and talk to you two."

"That is great, what did they have to say? Maybe we should wait for Cal and then you won't have to repeat it twice."

Cal came in the door while they were talking. Jackson told him about the representative from the rodeo association.

"Okay here is what the conversation was about. Because they know Jackson and all the championships, he has won they are very interested in him becoming a part of the NRA. They want to use Jackson and his accomplishments as part of the advertising for the rodeos we hold here. They are willing to pay for the use of any advertising we do. I told them we would have to discuss it and let their representative know of our decision after we talk to him about our plans for the ranch. The two of you need to think about what you want to do before the man comes tomorrow. He is due to be here about 10 am."

"Honey what do you think about it? Is it the right thing seeing that I am preaching? I guess we need to do some praying about it. I guess maybe I should talk to Jeff about it tonight. I don't want what I decide to do to effect either the Church or the Youth Ranch."

"Jackson, I don't see where it would affect either, but I do think you should talk to Jeff and you and Cal should discuss how far you want to go with all of this. Cal what are your thoughts?"

"I am like Barbara; I don't see why it should effect your preaching. I'm sure Jeff will be better qualified to advise you about it though. When everyone comes tonight, we can discuss it. It might be a good idea to get the opinions of Hank and Tom. We will need some legal advice from Tom anyway."

When the guys left the office, they talked a little about what Barbara told them.

"Jackson, it looks like the rodeo business is a go regardless of whether you want to be used in the advertising of it."

"I guess so, unless they use it as a stipulation for the certification. I guess we will just have to wait until we talk to him tomorrow."

Chapter Thirteen

When they got to the house, Barbara went in to see if Joyce needed help with dinner. She told her everything was taken care of. Cookie came over and helped her get it ready.

Everyone showed up at 6:00 and they sat down to eat. Jackson asked Jeff to say grace.

After dinner they went in the family room to talk.

"We have decided to get married on the 9th of December instead of the 29th. Cal and Gloria will get married on the 2nd. They will wait until after our wedding to go on their honeymoon".

Everyone asked what they could do to help get everything ready for both weddings. After they talked about the wedding plans Jackson filled them in on the Rodeo and what they have planned. He told them about the indorsement and advertising the association was wanting. He asked Jeff what he thought about it and how it would affect his preaching or if it would. Jeff told him he didn't see any problem as long as he made sure what is in his contract.

"Tom, I will have you look over the contract before I sign anything. I don't want to be obligated to anything if it would undermine my faith."

"I will be honored to look it over for you. We will make sure it is in keeping with what you are doing here and will not affect anything you do with the Church and Youth Camp."

"Jackson, we are all happy you and Barbara are getting married sooner. We will do anything you need in order to make it easier on the both of you."

"Thank you, Meredith. I knew we could count on all of you to help. We are planning a small wedding with just our family and close friends. The house will already be decorated for Cal and Gloria's wedding. There shouldn't be a lot to do here at the house. The wedding itself will be what we will need help with."

They talked about what each of them could do to help and they said their good-byes.

"Jackson, everyone is so good about helping. I love all of them so much. I never had a family like this before."

"Jasper will be here tomorrow. He is coming sooner so he will be here for the rodeo this weekend. He will be thrilled we have moved the wedding up."

They went in the den to have their devotions. They thanked God for their family and friends and the blessings he gives them each day. Jackson walked Barbara to her apartment. He gave her a kiss and told her it wouldn't be long before she wouldn't have to leave him.

When Barbara entered the house the next morning Joyce told her how happy she was they were getting married sooner. She would be happy to help in any way she could.

Barbara thanked her and told her when she hires the caterers for Cal and Gloria's wedding to be sure to have them come the next weekend for theirs and also the cleaning people.

"Joyce, we don't want you to tire yourself out with all of this. You will be baking both cakes and over-seeing everything. That is enough for you to handle. I want you to enjoy yourself."

Jackson and Cal came in for breakfast. Jackson came over and gave her a kiss and asked her what time the representative from the rodeo association was going to be there.

"He made an appointment for 10:00 this morning. I'll call your phone when he gets here if you are working."

"We'll try to be there when he gets here. I have to go out to the bull pasture and check on them right after breakfast. Davis and Chad will be delivering the cattle to Roanoke this morning."

"Barbara, Gloria is off today and will be out this afternoon to talk to you about our wedding if you have time."

"Cal, I will make time. Tell her to come to the office when she gets here. We have a lot to do in the next two weeks for your wedding and then I will only have a week to get ready for ours."

Barbara left to go out to the office. Marisa and Shirley were both there.

"Marisa, did you get anything done at your house yesterday. I'm sorry I didn't have a chance to come help you."

"I got a lot done. Did you get everything taken care of last night? I'm sure everyone is happy to help with your wedding. Let me know what I can do to help. If you need time off here, I will be happy to fill in for you. My work right now is light."

"Thank you, there will be times I will be out of the office. Shirley, there will be a representative from the rodeo association coming this morning. Please show him in to my office when he arrives and see if he would like coffee."

The rep from the rodeo association arrived right at ten. Shirley showed him in and brought him a cup of coffee. Barbara greeted him and then called Jackson to let him and Cal know he was there.

"Hi, I am glad to be here. My name is Jerry Porter. I have followed Jackson's time in the rodeo for years and am anxious to meet him."

"Jerry, I am Barbara Anderson. I am Jackson's fiancé. Jackson and Cal will be here in a few minutes. They are out checking on the bulls."

"Barbara, weren't you a barrel racer. You were in line for the Nationals when you left the rodeo. I often wondered what happened to you."

"It is a long story. I am back riding again. I have missed competing."

Jackson and Cal came in her office. Barbara introduced the men. He told Jackson he would like to look over everything and see what they have planned and where the rodeos would be held.

"Jerry lets go take a walk then and we will discuss everything while we are walking. Barbara, I think you should come with us in case we need any information about the finances involved."

While they were walking, Jackson told him they have someone interested in building a restaurant on the property. He showed him where they marked out for the buildings. Jerry told him he likes their plans.

"Jackson, you have a great place here for the rodeos. I like the idea of a restaurant on the property. Will you be holding Junior Rodeos? Seeing you have the Youth Ranch here I think it would be a great idea. Barbara, if I take some pictures, could you write us out a description of what each area will be used for. Maybe you could have your architect draw something showing us how everything will go together."

"I am sure we can get Brad to do what you need. Take the pictures and I will write you a description to go with them and when Brad gets the drawings done, I will overnight them to you."

"Jackson, I have the contract for you from the association. They want to use you and your championships in the advertisement for the ranch. I will leave them for you to look at and make any changes you need to. The sooner you can get it done and back to us the sooner we can release the money to help get this up and running I look forward to working with you. I was a great admirer of yours."

"I will have my lawyer look over the contract right away. I can't have anything in it affecting my running of the Youth Ranch and my being a pastor of our Church here."

"I understand and I can assure you, nothing will be asked of you in anyway undermining you as the person you are. It is all in your favor. We all respect you greatly."

"I appreciate it, but I am just a sinner like everyone else. I am just saved by God's grace. I will get this contract back to you as soon as Tom looks it over. Barbara will get the other information to you as soon as Brad can get the plans drawn up. Now how about joining us for lunch?"

"I would love to. Thank you so much and I think you are going to have a great place here."

The men left and went to the house. Barbara called Brad and asked him if he could come out to the ranch. They have some things they need to talk to him about and work they need him to do. He told her he would be there at 2:00. She thanked him and went to eat lunch. She told Marisa and Shirley to lock up and come to the house for lunch.

"Jackson, Brad is coming out at two. Can you be available or do you want me and Cal to handle it?"

189

"I will be here honey. Cal can you be here to? We need to both be sure of where we want everything to go."

"Do you want me to call Tom or will you take care of it? Jerry, I will work on the report you want this afternoon. Have you taken the pictures you want? I can put them in my computer and work them into my report if you would like."

"Barbara, it would be great. There are a few more I would like to take and then I will bring them to your office.

"Sweetheart, I will call Tom and invite him and Ellen to dinner. We can talk about the contract while you, Gloria and Ellen talk about the wedding."

Jerry brought the pictures to the office and Barbara loaded them in her report for him to take back with him. He thanked her and said he would be watching for the plans from Brad.

"Jerry, I will send them to you as soon as Brad has them done."

Brad came in the office a little before two. Barbara called Jackson and told him he was there. When Jackson and Cal come in the office, they explained to Brad what they would need. They all went out to look at the area where everything would be. He told them he would need to take some pictures in order to get everything in the right places.

"Brad, come back in the office and I will show you the pictures and report I just did for the association. I think they will help you with what you are needing."

"Barbara these are great. I can use this to draw my plans. I can probably have it back to you tomorrow. So, Jackson, you are going to do it. I have a feeling it will be great."

"It looks like it is going to be a go. Tom is coming out tonight to look over the contracts. How are you and Meredith coming along with your wedding? I didn't think to ask her the other night if she needed me to do anything for her."

"We will get with you and Jeff after your wedding and talk about ours. Jeff is going to officiate as you are giving her away. We have time to get everything settled when you and Cal are both back from your honeymoons. I'm glad you decided to move your wedding up."

"I guess four years is long enough to wait. I intended to ask her four years ago. God had a different idea about it though. We are both ready for marriage now. More than we would have been then."

Tom and Ellen arrived at 6:00 for dinner. When Davy saw Barbara, he ran to her and said he missed her. She gave him a hug and told Davy she missed him too.

Cal and Gloria came in and they all went in to eat. After the meal the men went into Jackson's office to look over the contract and the girls went in the den to talk about the flowers for the weddings.

"I'll bring in some potted plants as well as the fresh flowers. I can take the fresh ones with me after Gloria's wedding and put them in the cooler at the shop. Then I can replace any needing to be, before I bring them back for Barbara's wedding. We can leave up most of the decorations for the week. We just need to agree on the flowers you both want and the decorations. If you want different things then I will also make it work. It is up to the two of you."

They looked at the sample books Ellen brought with her and found out they both have pretty much the same ideas. They agreed on things they both liked.

The men came in and asked how things were going. They told them they were done. Joyce came in and asked if they would like dessert now and coffee. They told her thank you and they would clean up after so she could call it a night.

"How did you come out with the contract? Is everything okay? I will send it to them along with Brad's plans when they are both ready."

"Honey, Tom says the contract is good just the way they have it written. It pretty much protects both me and them. The amount they are willing to pay me for the advertising will guarantee us a good income to keep the rodeo going for a long time. With the revenue from the tickets we won't have any trouble building everything we need."

"Well it looks like you need to talk to Don as soon as Brad gets the plans done. It looks like Marisa and I will need to build some accounting programs for the rodeo. We are going to have a busy year."

Tom and Ellen left to take Davy home for bed. Cal told them he and Gloria were going over to their house and do some work.

Jackson and Barbara went in to clean up the dishes and went in the den to do their devotions. After they had their talk with God they decided to go on the porch and talk.

"Honey, are you okay with everything going on here at the ranch?"

"Of course, I am. This is what you have been working for. Between the four of us and God, we can make it everything you and Cal want it to be. We are all partners in this. Have you heard from Jasper? I thought he was going to be here today."

"He called when we were in the office. He had to take care of some business today and couldn't leave as early as he wanted. He said he would be here tomorrow."

"I'm glad he called; I was getting worried about him. I know he doesn't like to drive in the mountains at night."

Jackson walked her to her apartment and went back to the house. He thought how happy he was about the way things were going. He thanked God for all the blessings he bestowed on them.

The next morning Brad called Barbara and told her he would have the drawings ready for her today. He will bring them over when they are done, for Jackson and Cal to look at.

"Marisa, we need to work on an accounting program for the rodeo. It will probably be a little complicated. It will not only have to take care of the money paid out and taken in by the rodeo. It will also have to be able to take care of the fees paid by the riders and the money paid out to them and taken in by the concession stands. We may want to see if it will be better to separate them. I want you to work on it and then we will go over it together. You are so good at building the programs."

"I will start working on it right away and then we can see how it will work. Thank you for having so much faith in me."

"Marisa, you are so good at what you do. I just feel so blessed having you working with me."

"Thank you, I am so thankful God sent me here the day you ran your ad. I feel like this is where I am supposed to be with people who feel like family to me."

"Marisa, you are family. We are so thankful to have you here with us."

Shirley buzzed her and said Brad was there to see her. She told her to send him in and call Jackson to let him know Brad is here.

"Hi Barb, I have the plans for Jackson and Cal to look at. It is going to be quite a place when it is all finished. I showed them to

Dad and he said he would hire as many men needed to get it all done as soon as possible."

"Thank you Brad, we really appreciate you doing this so fast. The association is wanting it as soon as possible."

Jackson and Cal came in the office and shook hands with Brad. They all looked over the plans. Brad had even incorporated the restaurant in an area on the edge of the ranch. He told them they could have him move it where they want it if this doesn't work.

"Brad, I think it is the ideal place for it. People can come to the restaurant even when there are no rodeos and it will not interfere with the ranch in anyway."

"That is what I was thinking when I put it there. You can talk it over with the fellow wanting to build it. I figured you have about five acres there to work with."

"Barb, give Marc a call and ask him and his Dad out to the ranch to talk about the restaurant. Let me know when they can come out. Let him know we are going ahead with the Association rodeo."

Barbara put in a call to Marc and went to tell Jackson they would be out in the morning around nine. He gave Barb the plans Brad brought and told her to go ahead and overnight them to the Rodeo Association.

"Honey, ask them to okay them as soon as possible as we have the contractor ready to start when they are ready."

"I will send them immediately and let them know they are on the way. I will put a letter in it."

The next day Barbara heard back from the association and they gave them the go ahead. They loved the plans and looked forward to seeing everything up and running in the next few months. They said they would send someone out to talk to Jackson about the advertisement.

Barbara called Jackson and told him what they said. He told her to call Brad and have him start on the blueprints for all the new buildings and have his dad start as soon as they were ready.

"Barbara, I already started on the blueprints when I drew the plans. Dad will have his ground crews ready to set the foundations as soon as I have them finished, if we don't get a freeze."

"Thank you and tell your dad we appreciate everything you guys do for us. It seems like we keep you from taking on any other business. We just finish one thing before we are working on another."

Jackson came in the office just as she hung up the phone. She filled him in on her conversation with Brad. Shirley buzzed her and told her Marc and his father were there to see Jackson and Cal. She told her to send them in. She called Cal and asked him to come to the office.

"Marc, I'm glad you could come out so soon. Marshall, how are you? It has been awhile since I have seen you."

"Jackson, we are interested in what you have decided. I am glad to hear you are going ahead with the rodeo. What have you decided about the restaurant?"

"That is what we want to talk to you about. Barb will you get the plans Brad drew up for us."

When Barbara got out the plans. They showed Marc and Marshall where they were talking about putting a restaurant and why. He told them it looked like an ideal place to him.

"Jackson, decide on the lease amount and let me know when we can start building. I have all the financing arranged. I had a feeling we would be doing it."

Marshall told Jackson he would be interested in being involved in the rodeo part of the business. He is a silent partner with his son in the restaurant business.

"Marshall, I have a feeling we are going to need all the help we can get from people who know the rodeo like you do. When we have everything going in the planning stage, I will get with you. We have the okay from the association and I have the architect working on the blue prints. The contractor is ready to go when they are ready."

"Jackson, who is the architect and contractor you use? I like what he did with these plans and I would like to talk to him."

"They are a father and son team. Brad is engaged to my sister. You couldn't find a better team to work on it. Barbara will give you their phone number and address. It is 'Price and Sons construction company.'

"Jackson, seeing you are leasing me five acres, what would you think about me putting a motel next to the restaurant?"

Cal came in and Jackson introduced him to Marshall. They filled him in on what they were talking about. They decided on a lease amount for the five acres the Restaurant and parking area will be on. Jackson told them he would have his lawyer draw up the agreement and let them know when it is ready to sign.

"Marc, I have no objections to you doing a motel. It would be a good idea to have one close during the season. I have a feeling it would be good for the area year-round. The closest one right now is outside of Roanoke."

"I will talk to your architect and have him add it to the restaurant plans."

When Marc and his dad left, Jackson and Cal talked about everything. They knew they were going to be really busy when they got home from their honeymoons.

"Cal, you do know your wedding is just a little over two weeks away. We all need to start thinking about the weddings now and let the rest wait for a while. Everything is as far as we can get it for now."

"Jackson, we need to go get our suits this week. We can use the same ones for both weddings. You girls need to go get your dresses. We want you both to be married in wedding gowns. You can go to the same place Rhonda got hers. It was beautiful."

"We have already talked about going Monday as Gloria is off work. I will get my maid of honor dress at the same time."

"Barb, I think I just saw Jasper's truck pull up to the house. We need to go welcome him and get him settled in. Tell the girls to come to the house for lunch."

Barbara went out to the receptionist area and told Shirley and Marisa to come to the house for lunch. She told them she was going over there now to see Jasper and get him settled in the house.

"Marisa, don't forget the rodeo this weekend. The next couple of weeks are really going to be busy."

When they got to the house Joyce had gotten Jasper a cup of coffee and they were sitting at the table talking.

"Jasper we are so glad to see you. I hope you had a good trip."

"I am happy to be here. It was a nice easy trip, but I am glad to be here now. I have some things in the trailer I wanted to keep. I will need a place to park the trailer, until I find a house to buy. I would like to have a couple of acres so I can have a horse or two. I don't think I could live in town and not have horses to take care of."

"Jasper, we are so happy to have you here. Take your time finding a place to buy. I will put your trailer in the garage. It will be fine there for however long you need to keep it there. You know we will be happy to have you stay with us as long as you want."

"I appreciate your taking me in, but I need my own place. I plan on finding it here in Hidden Valley. I love it here and you two are like the children I never had. Now tell me about this rodeo you are going to have here."

Cal, Marisa and Shirley came in for lunch. Jackson introduced Shirley to Jasper. He told her she couldn't work for better people. She told him she already knew it.

Jackson said grace and they visited while they ate lunch. When lunch was over, they went back to work. Jackson helped Jasper bring his things to his room and then he went out to talk to Cal about moving the cattle the next day out to the open range.

Barbara asked Marisa to come to her office when they got back to the office.

"Marisa, do you think you can handle things for a couple of days? Gloria and I need to go look at dresses and I have some things I need to take care of before Cal and Gloria's wedding."

"Take off as much time as you need. If I need to talk to you about anything, I will call you. Shirley is a big help and I will be working on the programs for the rodeo. Everything else is caught up and nothing is pending, I can't take care of."

"Thank you so much. I will make sure all my work is done before I leave tonight. I don't know what I would do without you. God knew what he was doing when he sent you here to work with me."

Chapter fourteen

Barbara and Gloria headed to Roanoke to look at wedding dresses and a maid-of-honor dress. They both found what they wanted and decided to go have lunch at a restaurant.

"Gloria, what do you say we go look at shoes while we are here. Is there anything else you need?"

"What a great idea. I would like to go look at some jewelry. I don't normally wear jewelry so I don't have anything to go with a wedding dress."

"You know what? I'm like you, I don't have anything to wear either. When are your parents and little boy going to be here? What is his name. I don't think Cal has said."

"They will be here tomorrow. My dad called this morning and said they are on the way. My son's name is Mitchel. We call him Mitch. He just turned five last month."

"I bet he will love the ranch. Has he ever been around horses?"

"No, but he keeps talking about them ever since he found out we will be living on a ranch. My folks will stay at the house with him while we go on our honeymoon. My dad is a doctor."

"He will fit right in here then. I will be happy to meet them and Mitch."

The girls got home just in time for dinner. They told everyone they had gotten everything they went for. Jackson told them he and Cal went into Roanoke too. They got their suits. It looked like everything is getting done right on time.

"Cal, my folks will be here tomorrow. Maybe we should go to the house and make sure everything is ready for them."

"Okay honey, I think you are right. Jackson, I will see you in the morning. Davis and Chad got the cattle delivered okay. We will be ready to move the black angus to the open pasture in the morning."

"I'll see you in the morning. We will be ready to go right after chores. We should be back before dinner."

The next morning Barbara told Joyce they needed to talk about the rehearsal dinner on Friday night before the wedding. They decided on what to serve and Joyce told her the cleaning crew was coming in on Thursday, the caterers would be there at two on Friday. Gloria's parents arrived at eleven in the morning. Gloria brought them over to the house to meet Barbara. Joyce invited them to lunch.

Little Mitch wanted to go see the horses. Barbara told Gloria she would take him out to the stable. She needed to check on the horses with the men being gone.

Mitch wanted to pet the horses so Barbara brought Red out for him to pet. She asked him if he would like to sit on Red. He smiled and said "oh yes, can I?" Barbara picked him up and sat him on Red's back. He smiled so big Barbara couldn't help but laugh.

When they went in the house, he couldn't stop talking about riding the horse and petting him.

Gloria and her parents thanked her for taking him out there and letting him sit on the horse.

"It was fun. Red is a stallion, but as gentle as a puppy dog. He is my barrel racing horse. Jackson has several horses as gentle. He uses them with the youth who come to the ranch. Mitch will get a chance to learn to ride and take care of the horses. I have a feeling Cal will enjoy teaching him."

"When will we get to meet our future son and his brother? Gloria, your mother and I have been looking forward to being here. You have told us so much about everyone."

"Dad, they will be back in time for dinner. They had to move some cattle out to another pasture. They raise black angus cattle and they are kept on the open range. They don't feed them any feed with extra hormones or antibiotics in them."

"That is the kind of steak I like. Thank you, Joyce, for the wonderful lunch. Now we need to go and get settled in at Cal's house."

"Gloria, Mitch is welcome to stay with me while you get your folks settled. He can help me feed the horses. Would you like that Mitch?"

"Can I Mom? Can I stay with Aunt Barbara, I promise to be good and do what she tells me to do?"

"Okay you can stay but be sure to listen to your Aunt. I won't be long Barb."

"Take your time, don't forget I worked as a nanny for years on a horse ranch. We will have a good time."

When Gloria and her folks left, Barbara took Mitch and they went out to check the horses' water and hay. He was very good and did everything she told him to do. She let him put hay in the stalls for the horses. He thought he was a big boy now.

When Cal and Jackson rode back in to the yard Barbara and Mitch went out to great them.

Mitch went up to Cal and asked him if he was going to be his new Daddy.

"I sure am son. Can I have a hug? You are such a big boy. Where is your mother, granddad and grandma?"

Mitch jumped up into Cal's arms and gave him a hug. Cal had tears in his eyes. Jackson looked at them and smiled. He was happy for his brother. Now he has three nephews.

"Momma and grandma and grandpa are at our new house. I stayed with Aunt Barbara and helped feed the horses. She said I was a big help."

"I bet you were. Mitch this is your Uncle Jackson. He has been waiting to meet you."

"Hi there Mitch, can I have hug too. I have been waiting for you to come see us. You are a big boy and I bet you and Aunt Barbara had a good time."

Mitch gave him a hug and told him Aunt Barbara was a lot of fun. He liked her a lot.

Gloria and her folks drove up and she introduced them. They welcomed them to the ranch and family. Mitch, told them what he and his new aunt did all afternoon and how much he liked being here on the ranch.

"We will have a family dinner tomorrow night so you can meet the rest of the family. We decided tonight should just be us. The women can talk about the wedding and we can go in the den and get acquainted."

Joyce came out on the porch and told them dinner would be ready in a half hour. Cal told them he needed to go to his house and shower. He would be right back. Jackson excused himself to go take a shower too.

Barbara said she should go up to her apartment and get ready for dinner. "I will be right down. Why don't you take your parents in the house and show them around?"

Gloria took her parents and Mitch in the house and showed them the work Jackson had done. She told them they were going to have the wedding there in the large open room. She told them that it had been two rooms, but Jackson had them opened up into one.

"Gloria, they sure did a beautiful job on it. It looks like it has always been this way. How many acres does Cal and Jackson own here? It seems like they have a lot going on."

"They have Dad, but it is nothing to what it will be like. When they are done it will be almost like a town of its own. They have 1000 acres. Jackson raises rodeo livestock; he has the Youth Ranch and now they have got certified to hold NRA rodeos here.

They will build an outside arena, bathrooms and bunk houses. They have leased five acres to a restaurant owner who is going to build a restaurant and Motel on the west edge of the property."

"Are they partners in everything? It seems like they have accomplished an awful lot for as young as they are."

"Jackson, bought the ranch when he retired from the rodeo. When Cal left the marines, he came here to work with him. Jackson put him on the deed as a full partner. Cal invested some of his retirement in the ranch."

"I'd say he is a good brother to have. They don't look anything alike do they."

"They are both adopted. Their parents adopted five children. The only one's blood related, are Jeff and Jackson and they didn't know until recently they are blood brothers. You will meet all of them tomorrow night. Jackson has asked them all out for dinner. Did I tell you Jackson and Jeff are ordained ministers?

Jackson is going to officiate at the wedding and Jeff is going to be Cal's best man."

"When do they have time to take care of a Church? Didn't you tell me his brother Jeff is a pediatrician? This is quite a family you are marring into."

"They preach at a Spanish Church. They alternate Sundays. Jackson also relieves the minister at the Community Church when the pastor and his family need time off."

The men came in and Gloria's father told them she was filling them in on the family. He told them he has a lot of respect for all of them.

Jackson thanked him. He told him; they only do what God guides them to do. They couldn't do any of it without Him in their lives.

"We are happy to have you and Mrs. Taylor here and hope you enjoy your stay."

"Jackson, please call us Norman and Vera. This Mr. and Mrs. Stuff is for strangers not family."

Joyce came in and told them dinner was ready. They went into the dining room and Jackson said grace. They talked about the weddings in two weeks and the next week. Vera asked what she could do to help get everything ready.

"Mom everything is taken care of. We will go to the beauty parlor on Saturday morning and have our hair and nails done. Joyce has taken care of everything. The rehearsal dinner for our wedding will be on the Friday night before the wedding."

"Have you had a shower yet? The wedding is only two weeks away."

"The shower is next week at Jeff and Lora's home. You will love it. It is a beautiful Victorian home. It is on the historical society registry. Everyone has been so great about helping us when we moved the wedding up."

They went in the den to have their coffee and dessert. Jackson told Joyce to go enjoy her evening with George and they would take care of the dishes.

While they were talking, they heard a car pull up. Jackson went to the door. Jeff, Lora, Meredith, Brad and Beth were standing on the porch. They told him they came to meet Gloria's parents. He told them to come in.

Barbara told them to come in and sit down. She would go get them some coffee and dessert. Gloria, Meredith and Beth went to help her.

Cal introduced Gloria's parents to his family. He told them he was glad to meet them.

"We figured it would help if you folks got to meet us before tomorrow night when the rest of the crew get here. It's a little easier to meet a few at a time."

"You mean there is more in your family? I thought Gloria said there was just the five of you."

"This is all of the Barnes crew, but the rest of the bunch are as close as family. You will meet Hank Norton and his family, Tom Brown and his wife and son and the Price family who are Brad and Anna's parents and her brother and his family."

"I understand Jeff, you and your wife are both doctors. I am a General Practitioner. I wanted my daughter to be a doctor, but she likes being a surgical nurse. I tried to get her to come home to practice, but I guess it is just as well she didn't."

"I'm a pediatrician and Lora's an obstetrician. Hank Norton who you will meet tomorrow night is a Neuro Surgeon and his wife Anna is also a Surgical Nurse as well as head of Nursing at the hospital."

"I believe I know Dr. Norton. I met him at a convention I attended and he was the key speaker. He is quite famous."

"He is, but you would never know it to talk with him here at home. He bought the hospital here when it was going to be torn down and brought it back to life."

"I would love to visit the hospital after the wedding and while we are still here."

"I am sure it can be arranged. You will enjoy your stay here. The thing about the Valley is once you come here you don't want to leave."

Jasper came in while they were talking. Barbara asked him where he has been. He told her he ate dinner with the men. He hadn't had a chance to catch up with them since he got there. She introduced him to Gloria's parents and asked if he would like some coffee or dessert. He thanked her and said he was tired from his trip and thought he would go up to bed. They told him good-night and he left.

"Jasper, don't forget the rodeo is this weekend. You are going with us?"

"I will come on Sunday with Jackson. I wouldn't miss seeing you ride again."

Everyone said their good-nights and Barbara and Gloria took everything out to the kitchen to wash them. Gloria's mother came in and helped them. She told them Mitch has fallen asleep in the room where the children were playing. Cal come in and told Gloria they needed to get her parents and Mitch home so they could get some rest. The rest of the week was going to be busy. He told her she could spend the night in the extra guest room. He didn't want her driving home this late.

When the others left, Jackson came in the kitchen to help Barbara finish up. He gave her a kiss and told her just three more weeks and they would be married. She told him it was going to go fast with everything they have to do in the next two weeks for Cal and Gloria's wedding.

"Honey, with the rodeo this weekend and you preaching this Sunday we are going to be short a few days. The girls will be out tomorrow and Thursday to practice. They will spend the night Thursday night so we can leave early Friday morning. This way you can get us there and get home early in the afternoon."

"Sweetheart, I wish I could be there with you for the weekend. You will do great. Ramona and Rand will follow us back here on Sunday. Let's get you home so you can get some rest. Have I told you lately how much I love you?"

"I love you too. I thank God every night for bringing us together again."

Jackson walked her to her apartment and gave her a sweet kiss good night. On the walk back to the house he thanked God for all the blessings he has given them this year.

The next morning Barbara went in the office to make sure she didn't have anything she needed to take care of before the weekend.

"Barbara, I have everything under control and if we need you, we will call You."

"I have everything ready to leave on Friday for the rodeo. I am looking forward to going with you and the girls and watching you ride."

"We will be leaving early Friday morning. Maybe you should spend the night here on Thursday night."

"I will bring my clothes to work with me Thursday. We will all have a good time. I haven't been to a rodeo in years. My husband and son loved to go. I am looking forward to going and watching the barrel racing mostly."

"I will be working in the arena with Red. If you need me give me a call. The girls are coming out after school to work with their horses."

Barbara went out to work with Red. Gloria's dad came in the arena and was watching her. When she finished her run, she saw him standing by the gate. "Barbara, I have never seen a better run. I have gone to a lot of rodeos, but you are about the best rider I have ever seen."

She thanked him and said it was because she has a great horse.

The girls came in the arena and Barbara told them to get their horses saddled while she put Red away. They all left to go to the stable.

When the girls were finished working with their horses, Barbara said, "when you come out tomorrow night bring your clothes with you so you can stay the night. We will leave early on Friday morning for the rodeo grounds."

"Don't forget to let the school know you will not be there on Friday. Have them call me if they need verification of where you will be."

Jackson came to the arena just as Barbara was getting ready to leave.

"Hi honey, how did everything go. Are you ready for the rodeo? I saw the girls leaving a minute ago."

"They did great. I told them to bring their things tomorrow night. They will spend the night here. Marisa is going to stay too, so we can get an early start Friday morning."

"Marisa and the girls can ride in the motor home with us. Jasper is going to follow us and bring me back. We will help you get set up and I'll get the girls registered for their classes."

"Great, I'm glad Jasper is coming and driving you home. It will be a good time for the two of you to talk about the rodeo you will be holding at the ranch."

"We do have a lot to talk about. He wants to invest in the rodeo and Youth Ranch."

"I need to go get cleaned up for dinner. Everyone will be here in a couple of hours."

When Barbara came in the house, Gloria and her parents were there. Mitch came running over to Barbara and gave her a hug. Barbara asked him if he was having fun in his new home.

"I love it here Aunt Barbara. My new daddy told me he is going to teach me how to ride the horses. He said he will get me a horse of my own."

"That is wonderful Mitch. We all love having you here with us. You will get to meet some more children to play with tonight."

When everyone arrived, Cal introduced Gloria's parents to them. Shane walked over and took Mitch's hand. He introduced him to the rest of the children. He had played with Mitch the night before.

Gloria's dad and Hank got to talking about the hospital and how they had made it into one of the best hospitals in the county.

"Hank I would love to see it."

"Norman I would love for you to stop by tomorrow. I will show you around."

Joyce called them all in for dinner. Jeff said the blessing and they continued their conversation while they ate. After dinner the men went to the den to talk. The women went in the family room to talk about the weddings.

Later Joyce brought their dessert and coffee to the family room and Barbara went to tell the men it was there. The men came in to join them.

The older boys had gone to the play room with the little ones, so Joyce took their dessert in to them. When she came back out Jackson told her to go spend the evening with George and they would take care of everything now.

When they got through with their dessert the women went in the kitchen to clean everything up. The kids all came in with the parents.

"Momma and Daddy, I had so much fun. I have a lot of cousins now to play with."

The adults smiled and told him he has all kinds of aunts, uncles and cousins.

When everyone left for the night, Jackson and Barbara sat in the den and talked about what they needed to do the next two weeks after the rodeo to get ready for their wedding.

"Honey, I think everything is pretty well taken care of now. By having our wedding right after Cal and Gloria's we won't have much to do."

"Darling, I am so glad we decided to do it this way. It makes it a lot easier on you and we get to be married sooner."

Jackson walked her to the apartment and gave her a kiss and told her good-night.

The next morning when Marisa got to the office Barbara took her up to the house and showed her to the guest bedroom.

"Barbara the house is beautiful. I love the big open room downstairs."

"I love it too. Jackson had it done after we decided to get married. We are having Cal, Gloria, Jackson and my weddings there. Ellen will be decorating it for both weddings."

"I know it will be beautiful. I guess I had best get out to the office or Shirley will think she is on her own today as well as tomorrow."

"I will be out there in a little while. We can fill her in on what to do tomorrow while we are both gone."

Marisa left and went to the office. Barbara went out to the stable to check on Red and get her equipment ready for the rodeo.

The girls would be out after school to get their horses and saddles ready. She was having them stay in her guest room in her apartment tonight.

When she had everything ready, she went to the office to talk to Shirley and Marisa.

"Shirley all you will need to do is answer the phone and if there is anything important let Jackson or Cal know. They will take care of it."

"You know you are both invited to the weddings."

Jackson came in the office and asked if there was anything, he could do to help them get ready for tomorrow.

"Everything is under control. Shirley will call you or Cal if something comes up tomorrow, she can't handle."

Barbara went out to ride Red. While she was riding, Gloria came up with Mitch.

"Aunt Barbara can I ride with you?"

She rode over to the gate and Gloria handed him to her. She rode around the arena with him in front of her. She gave him the reins and showed him how to hold them and guide Red around the arena. She thought how much fun it was going to be to have this little boy here.

Cal came in the arena and saw Mitch on the horse. He thought how great Barbara is with kids. He hoped she and Jackson will have a house full. They both loved kids. He hoped he and

Gloria will have more children too. He loves this little boy and always will but would like to have more. No child should have to grow up alone. If God is willing, this ranch will be filled not only with the kids from the Youth Ranch, but with children of their own.

Barbara took Mitch back to his mother and told him she has to get Red ready for the rodeo tomorrow night.

"Can I help you Aunt Barbara?" "Gloria leave him with me if you want to."

"Barbara are you sure he won't be in the way? I know you have a lot to do today."

"He will be okay. He is good about doing what I tell him. We will have a good time. You go enjoy your parents. Maybe you can talk Cal into taking some time off to be with you all."

Barbara and Mitch gave Red a bath. He thought it was fun. Then they brushed him down and cleaned his stall and put in fresh bedding. Jackson came in the stable and asked if he could help. She told him she has a really good helper. He smiled at Mitch.

The girls showed up to ride. They told Mitch, "hi, how do you like living on the Ranch?"

"I love it. Aunt Barbara has been teaching me how to ride. My new dad is going to give me a horse of my own."

They told him they would see him later. They needed to get their horses ready for the rodeo too.

Barbara took the girls to her apartment when they got done riding. Then they got ready to go have dinner. When dinner was over the girls played with Mitch for a while. When Cal and Gloria left to go back to Cal's house, the girls went up to the apartment.

Jackson and Barbara went in the den to do their devotions and spend some time with God and each other.

"Honey we will leave around six in the morning. I guess I'd best walk you to your apartment so you can get some rest. I am going to miss you this weekend. I'll be glad when Sunday gets here so I can come and see you ride."

"I will miss you too. When you start having the rodeos here, I think I will just ride in them. I really am not interested in trying to make nationals. I will let Ramona take care of that. I will be satisfied with riding here."

He walked her home and kissed her good-night. Barbara went in thinking how lucky she was to have him in her life again. She knew God had plans for their lives. She could hardly wait to start their life together as husband and wife.

Jackson, thanked God for bringing them together again after all these years. He thought to himself it was true all things work out for those who wait on the Lord.

Chapter Fifteen

Jackson drove them to the Harrisonville rodeo the next morning in the motor home and set it up for them. Jasper pulled in right after they got done. Jackson went to register them for the barrel racing Friday night. He signed the girls up for Sunday afternoon and evening. He told them to enjoy the rodeo on Saturday with Marisa and the other girls.

When he had everything taken care of, he told them he needed to get back to the ranch, but Davis and George would be there in a couple of hours with the broncs and bulls. If they need anything to let the men know. Davis would be checking in on them later. He and George were planning on watching them ride tonight.

Ramona showed up an hour later and put her horse in his stall. Barbara introduced her to the girls.

"Ramona, are you and Rand still following us to the ranch on Sunday?"

"We sure are. We are looking forward to seeing the ranch and talking to Jackson some more about the Rodeo Camp."

"Ramona, Jackson has been certified to have NRA rodeos at the ranch. He is building a large outdoor arena and a lot of other buildings. There is also going to be a restaurant and motel on the west side of the property."

"Wow! Things sure change fast with you two, don't they? When did all of this happen? It has only been a week since we saw you."

"We started checking into it right after we got home. Jackson will finish his contract with the rodeos for this year and then he will use his livestock for the rodeos on the ranch. I will barrel race at our rodeos, but I don't plan on competing in any others."

"What about the nationals? You will be a contender for the championship."

"I really don't care to win the nationals. I just like to compete for my own satisfaction. I'll leave the nationals to you."

"It won't be near as much fun as trying to beat you. You always make me work harder when you compete against me. I have missed you the last four years. I already have three championships. I was hoping you would win this year."

"I appreciate it, but I am happy the way things are. It would have been nice if I hadn't messed up when I was younger, but now it really isn't important to me. I just want to help Jackson with his dream and do what God has for me to do."

That night when the barrel racing was over Barbara had won first place, Ramona came in second by one second on her run.

The girls had come in fifth and sixth place. Barbara was so proud of them.

Davis and Chad came over to congratulate them all. Davis told Barb, "George decided to stay home and sent Chad with me this time."

Chad was talking to Maria and Christina. He told them he was very proud of them. Barbara thought Chad was just four years older than the girls. They all seemed to be enjoying each other's company.

The next two days were fun days for the girls. Marisa went with them to see the bull riders and bronc riders. She told them Ramona's husband was one of the bull riders. He won first place. It put him in the running for nationals.

Ramona got first place on Saturday afternoon and they tied for first on Saturday evening. Sunday afternoon Barbara decided not to ride. She would ride Sunday evening. Sunday afternoon Ramona won first and the girls won fourth and fifth places.

Jackson and Jasper arrived a couple of hours before the final competitions of the rodeo. Barbara was glad they made it before time for their rides.

"Hi sweetheart, how have things gone? How have the girls done?"

"They have done great for their first rodeo. I am very proud of them. By next year they will be in the running for some first-place wins. I think Ramona will be up for Nationals."

"Are you sure you don't want to try for Nationals this year? You know we will go to any rodeos you want to enter."

"Honey I know you will take me to any I want to enter, but I will be just as happy riding in our rodeos. I don't need to win Nationals to make me happy. I love just doing it when I can. I will be glad if in a couple of years one of the girls win it."

When the rodeo was over Rand was up for Nationals and so was Ramona. They congratulated them and told them they would be ready to leave for the ranch in about an hour.

Ramona had won first again and Barbara second by one second. They were both happy with the way the rodeo ended.

Jackson went to help load the livestock and then came back to get the trailer hooked up to the motor home and load the horses.

Rand and Ramona pulled up beside them with their truck and horse trailer. Marisa and the girls decided to ride back with Jasper in the SUV so Jackson and Barbara were alone in the motorhome. Jackson asked her if she would like to take the motorhome on their honeymoon. She told him it would be great. They could just go wherever they wanted to and not worry about being at a certain place at a certain time.

When they got to the ranch Jackson took Rand out to the new stable to put his horses up. Barbara and the girls took their horses to the stable to feed and water them.

When the horses were taken care of, they went to the house. Joyce had left coffee and desert out for them. Jackson and Rand took their suitcases up to the guest room. Marisa and the girls had left for home. When Jackson and Rand came downstairs the four of them went in the den to drink their coffee and talk. Jasper had already gone to his room. He told them good-night, he was ready for bed.

"Jackson, you have a great place here. I want to look for a ranch something like this, but not as big. We would like to find about five acres and a house."

"We can talk to Don Price about it. He knows every place for sale in the area. He has the largest construction company in the state. He has done all my construction. His son Brad is engaged to my sister Meredith and Brad is one of the best architects in the country."

"I want to look over your place tomorrow. You have 1000 acres here. Where do you plan on having the rodeo set up? I notice you already have a large indoor arena. Have you planned on an outdoor arena too? You have a great place here for everything."

"I have the plans for the compound in the office. Tomorrow I will show it to you. Brad drew a plan showing everything and

217

how it will look. We can go out there in the morning and you will get a better idea of how it will look."

They all said good-night and Jackson walked Barbara to her apartment. He kissed her and told her he would see her in the morning.

The next morning, they all went to breakfast and Barbara went to the office to check on things. Marisa and Shirley greeted her when she came in. Shirley told her everything was good. There was nothing needing her attention this morning. Jackson and the others came in to look at the plans for the rodeo compound. They went in her office.

"Jackson, this is great. He makes it look just like you are right there. He even has the restaurant and motel in them. When do you think it will be up and running?"

"If the weather holds out Don says it should be ready in about nine months. The restaurant will be up and running in about six months. Do you remember Marshall Wade?"

"I sure do. He won almost as many championships as you did. He was one of the great, bull and bronc riders of his age."

"His son is the one building the restaurant. Marshall is a silent partner in the one in Roanoke. He wants to invest in the rodeo here."

"Do you think you will be taking in a lot of investors? It could become a problem with too many I would think."

"I will be very careful about who I let in. Jasper is investing in the rodeo. I am thinking about letting Marshall in too. I don't need too many investors. The NRA is paying me to use my picture and championship record for their advertisements. It is enough to get the construction we need done."

"Will this interfere with the Rodeo Camp you were thinking about starting. I have talked to a lot of riders who are interested in the camp."

"No, I am still hoping to have the camp going this next year. We will hold the camp between the rodeos. Barbara and Marisa are busy getting the financials set up for both the rodeo and the camp."

"I would like to be involved in any way I can. You are going to need all the help you can get to make everything move smoothly."

"I would be more than willing to hire both you and Ramona to help with the camp and rodeo. Let's go talk to Don Price about any property available for you. Barbara, would you like to go with us?"

"Marisa, are you alright with me leaving you girls alone again? I know you have been having to handle a lot for me recently."

"Get out of here. We are fine with it. You have a lot to get done in the next couple of weeks with Cal and your weddings. If we need you, we know how to reach you. Go enjoy yourselves."

Jackson called Don and asked if he had time to talk to them. He told them to come to the office. He was free this morning. He wanted to talk to him too.

When they got to the office Jackson introduced Rand and Ramona to Brad and Don. He welcomed them to Hidden Valley and asked what he could do for them.

"Rand and Ramona are interested in buying a small ranch in the area. I told them if there was one you would be the one to talk to."

"As a matter in fact there is a 10-acre ranchette about five miles out of town for sale. The owner has been transferred out of state and they are anxious to sell. Would you like to go look at it? I don't think it will last long. The home is only three years old. I built it and the stable."

"I would love to see it. We can go now if you have the time."

"I am ready if you are. Jackson, I can talk to you on the way out there."

"What did you want to talk about Don? How are things going with the permits for the rodeo ground?"

"That is what I wanted to talk to you about. We need to go before the county board with the plans for the rodeo. They have to approve the plans before the permits can be issued. We are scheduled for the next meeting. It is the week of your wedding. Do you want me to delay it?"

"Barbara, what do you think? If it is at the first of the week, I think it will be okay. Honey it is up to you."

"When is the meeting Don? I'm sure if it is on Monday or Tuesday it will work out okay. Jackson and Cal can attend it. If they need any financial information, I can give it to them to take."

"It is on Monday, so I think it will work out. I will let you know what they will need. Brad and I are both on the board and so is Tom so I don't see any problem. It is just something that has to be done to make it legal."

They arrived at the ranch. The house was a beautiful ranch style home with a porch that went all the way across the front. Ramona told them she loved it before she got out of the car. Rand laughed and said they may not get to look inside before she has it bought.

The owner came out and Don introduced them. They went in to look at the house. "It has four bedrooms, a den, living room, dining room, kitchen with an eat in area and three bath rooms."

Rand asked to go look at the stable and barn. He really liked the looks of the house. The stable was built with six stalls, an office, tack room and wash area for the horses. The barn held the hay and feed storage area. They went in the house to talk.

The rancher's wife had coffee and cookies for them. They agreed on a price and Jackson said he would take him to Tom's office to have a title search done and to draw up the deed. They told the rancher they would let him know when to meet them at Tom's office.

"Tom has already been working on the title, when he found out I would be selling it."

Jackson went ahead and called Tom. "Jackson the title is clear and I can have the deed ready for them tomorrow if they want me to. They can come to my office tomorrow morning at 10:00, if it is convenient for them."

Jackson asked them if it worked for them and they agreed.

"We will need a couple of weeks to get moved. Will it work okay for you folks?"

"That is fine. It will probably be that long or longer before we can get packed and ready to move ourselves. We live in Tennessee now. We have to give notice to our landlord about moving and pack up. Jackson, could we board our horses at your ranch until we move?"

"You can bring your horses here if you want. I don't mind taking care of them for you until you can get moved."

"Thank you, that would be great, if you don't think it will be too much on you while trying to get ready to move."

"It would be fine. I can feed them and open the doors into the paddock for them to exercise. They won't be any trouble."

They decided to meet at Tom's office the next morning. Rand told him he would bring a certified check for the purchase of the property. He just has to call his bank and have the money transferred to his checking account.

When they left the ranchette, Ramona told Don she loved the house. They thanked him for taking them out there. He told them he was glad things worked out for them.

Rand called his bank while they were driving back to town. They told him the money would be available in an hour. He thanked them and told Jackson he needed to go to the bank in Hidden Valley and set up an account with them and get the cashier's check for the property.

Barbara said they could take him to their bank. She could introduce them to Jackson's banker.

Don took them back to his office, to get their car and they went to the bank. When everything was done, they decided to stop for lunch. Barbara called Joyce and told her they were having lunch in town and not to wait on them.

When they got back to the ranch Barbara went to check in with Marisa.

"Barbara, the accounting program is ready for you to look at when you have time. Gloria wants you to call her."

She went in her office to call. They made plans to get together that evening with Gloria's mother to talk about the rehearsal dinner and the wedding. The shower was tomorrow night. The men were all going out for dinner while they had the shower. Ellen was coming in the morning along with Meredith to decorate for the shower.

"Barb, tell Ramona she is invited to the shower, the dinner and the wedding. We are glad you are going to be a part of the valley."

Ramona went out to ride her horse in the arena where the barrels were set up. Barbara came out and saddled Red and joined her. They were having fun when the men came out to watch them. Jackson told Rand they were like a couple of kids playing games. They laughed, Rand said he was glad they found the ranch so soon. They were glad they would all be close.

The girls went to take care of their horses and get ready for dinner. Joyce said Gloria and her parents were coming for dinner. Cal was already at the house. He was talking to the men about some decorating he wanted them to help with. They were going to put up the Christmas decorations outside before the wedding this weekend.

After dinner they went in the den to talk. They wanted to make sure everything was ready for the wedding. The girls took their dresses to the second master suite upstairs. They would dress there before the wedding. The men would dress in the downstairs master suite.

Joyce told them the cleaning crew was coming at 7:00 on Friday morning.

"Joyce, thank you so much for all the work you have done for us. You have helped make this a wonderful wedding in so short a time."

"We have an appointment on Saturday morning to have our nails and hair done. Tomorrow night is the shower and Wednesday we can actually take a breather."

When the rest had left, Jackson and Barbara sat in the den and talked. He told her Cal and the men were going to put the outside Christmas decorations up tomorrow.

"Honey, do you want to decorate the house before our wedding for Christmas? We can talk to Ellen and see what she thinks about it."

"I'll talk to her when she comes to decorate for the shower tomorrow night. I like the idea of a Christmas theme for our wedding. It will make it different from Cal and Gloria's if it isn't too much trouble for Ellen."

"Honey, don't worry if it is too much trouble. Ellen will be happy to do whatever you want for your wedding. It needs to be what you want it to be."

"I know, but it is such short notice. I don't want to cause any more work than necessary."

"We will help with the decorating. It won't be too much trouble."

Jackson walked her to her apartment and told her not to worry about the decorations tonight. She can talk to Ellen tomorrow when she and Meredith come to decorate for the bridal shower.

The next morning, when Barbara came in for breakfast Jackson and Cal were talking about the restaurant they were going to tonight while the girls had the bridal shower.

"Good morning. How is the future groom doing this morning? Just four more days to go."

"You would have to remind me. Now I am getting nervous. I just hope I can be the husband and father that God and Gloria want me to be."

"Cal, I have no doubt you will be a wonderful husband and father. God put the three of you together and he will be with you always."

"Thank you, Barb. You are going to be a great sister. I am so glad my big brother finally came to his senses."

"Good morning, darling. How are you this morning? I hope you slept instead of worrying about decorating for our wedding."

"I slept really well, once I gave it over to God to handle. I need to check in at the office and then I will be here to help Ellen and Meredith decorate."

Barbara went to the office and talked to Marisa and Shirley. They told her everything was fine there and for her to go do what she needed to and they would see her at the shower.

"Barbara, if anything comes up here, we will call you. Go help with the decorations and we will see you later."

"Thank you both. I will leave everything up to you then and see you tonight."

When she got back to the house Ellen and Meredith were there getting ready to work. She told them hello and asked if they would like some coffee and rolls before they got to work.

Ellen said, she would love some. They could go talk over the decorations before they start working on them.

"Barbara, I see the men are starting to put up the Christmas decorations outside. What would you think about changing the decorations for your wedding to a Christmas theme?"

"Ellen, I would love it. I was talking to Jackson last night. I was afraid it would be too much work for you on such short notice."

"Barb, it would not be too much work for me. You can all help decorate. Have Jackson get a large Christmas tree for the great room and I will take care of the rest."

"I told God I would leave it up to him. I guess He took care of it. Thank you so much. We will all help with the decorations. We have a week to get them done."

The girls got to work decorating for the shower. When everyone got there, they loved the way the house looked. The men came in and said they were going to Roanoke for dinner and for the girls to have fun.

The shower was still going on when the men came back.

"Cal, look at all the nice gifts we got."

"Gloria, they are all wonderful." He gave her a sweet kiss. "I will help you take everything to the house."

Her father and mother told her they would help.

"Gloria, leave Mitch here for the night. He has fallen asleep in the guest bedroom. Joyce said she would listen for him if he woke up in the night."

They all pitched in and helped load the presents into Cal's car. When everyone left Jackson and Barbara went in the den to talk.

"Jackson, Ellen brought up the idea of decorating the house with a Christmas theme for our wedding, before I could. I left it in God's hands and she brought it up when she got here this morning."

"I told you she would be alright with it. I knew she would want you to have the wedding you want."

"She wants you to get a large tree for the great-room. We will all get together to decorate the house next week. She said she would take care of everything else we will need."

"Would you like a real tree or a store bought one? Myself, I would like to have a real one. There is a grove of them in the pasture where the cattle are. If you want one, I will take one of the men with me to get it. It is up to you darling; I will get whatever you want."

"Honey, I would love to have a real tree. I would love to go with you to look for one. We could hook one of the draft horses up to the wagon and go for it."

"That sounds like a great idea. I saw a sleigh for sale in the farm magazine the other day. I wonder if it is still there. I would love to have one. We have the horses to pull it. It would be great for the Youth Ranch. It said it has wheels so we can use it without snow."

"Call and see if they still have it. We could go look at it tomorrow morning. Then we could go look for a tree. Where is it?"

"It is about 50 miles from here. It wouldn't take long to go after it if they still have it."

Jackson went to his office and got the magazine. He called the number. The man said he still had it. They made arrangement to go see it in the morning. He told Jackson he has a trailer he uses to carry it on. He would let him use it to haul the sleigh, if he decides to buy it. Jackson told him they would be there around eight in the morning.

"He still has it and we are meeting him at eight in the morning to look at it. We will need to take my truck to haul it home. He has a trailer we can use."

The next morning, they left early to go look at the sleigh. It was just what they wanted. Jackson bought it and asked the man if he would like to sell the trailer. He said he would if Jackson wanted it. Jackson paid him for both and they left for home.

When they got home, Cal came out of the stable and asked Jackson where he had gotten the sleigh. He told him he just bought it. He told him they could use one of the draft horses to pull it.

Friday the cleaning crew were at the house early. The rehearsal dinner was at Jeff and Lora's, the rehearsal went great.

"Well Cal, the big day is tomorrow brother. How are you holding up? Will we have to pick you up off the floor when you faint?"

"Thanks Jeff, you just made me feel so calm. Love you too big brother. I am fine, I will just be glad when tomorrow is over."

The next day was busy for everyone. The women went to get their hair and nails done. When they got home it was time to dress for the wedding. The house looked beautiful.

At 6:00 Gloria came down the stairs behind Barbara. They both looked beautiful, but Gloria took your breath away. She was a beautiful bride. Cal couldn't believe she would be his in just a few minutes.

Jackson started the wedding. He told everyone his Brother and his Bride wanted to say their own vows to each other.

"Gloria, you came in my life when I needed you most. You are my life. I will always love you and Mitch with all that is in me. With God in our lives we will be able to handle anything that comes our way. I love you both with all my heart."

"Calvin, you are my life and my true love. I will honor and love you forever we will always keep God in our life."

When he pronounced them husband and wife, everyone applauded while Cal kissed his bride. She was now his and Mitch was his son. He thanked God for her and Mitch and all the friends there for their wedding.

The chairs were moved and everyone watched the Bride and Groom dance. The rest of the family joined them.

After dinner Gloria and Cal skipped out and went to Roanoke to spend the weekend.

Chapter Sixteen

Monday morning Jackson went out to the stable to talk to Cal. He planned on going to the upper pasture and cutting their Christmas tree.

"Cal, we are going to the upper pasture and look for a Christmas tree for the house. Would you and Gloria like to go look for one, for your house?"

"Let me call her and see. She and her parents are at the house. How are you going to bring them back?"

"That is why I bought the sleigh. We can use the draft horses to pull it and bring them back on it. You and Gloria can ride your horses out."

Gloria and her dad said they would love to go. Barb told Jackson she would ride Red out there and Gloria's dad could ride on the sleigh with him. They all got ready to go. Joyce packed them a lunch. She told them they would be hungry before they got back from there.

"Jackson, the grove of pine trees is beautiful. It has so many large trees."

They found two, perfect for the houses. Cal and Jackson got busy cutting them. They brought some large burlap bag to wrap them with to protect the branches.

They loaded the trees and decided to eat their lunches before they headed back.

"Cal, the cattle are looking good. I'm glad we brought them back up here."

"Jackson, it is so beautiful up here. The mountain range makes a wonderful natural boundary for the cattle. It is even more beautiful than it was from the air."

"I have to agree with you. I love it up here. The trees and the mountains protect the cattle in the winter as long as we don't get too much snow. If we do, hay will have to be brought in to feed them. I really don't want to, if I can keep from it."

"Will we have to bring them back down to the ranch if it gets too much snow up here?"

"We will just have to wait and see. They have lived up here for two years with no help from humans. I think they should be alright."

They left to take the trees back to the ranch. They stopped at Cal's and unloaded his tree. Gloria told him they needed to get a stand for it and decorations before they can put it up. They put it in the garage until they could go to town.

"Jackson, we need to go after a stand and decorations too. I need to ask Ellen what she wants us to get for it. We can take the tree out to the barn until I talk to Ellen."

Barbara called Ellen and told her about the tree.

"Barbara I will be out in a while to look at the tree. I will get the decorations for everything. All you and Jackson need to do is get the tree set up. I will bring a stand with me when I come."

Barbara went to tell Jackson. "Sweetheart I will get the tree in the house when she gets there. We will get it in the stand for her."

"Hi Ellen, the tree is in the barn. It is large and fresh cut. We went to the upper pasture and cut them. Cal got one for their home too. I'll call Jackson and have him bring it in. Do you need help unloading your car?"

"I have a lot out there. Maybe we can get a couple of the men to unload it for us."

Barbara called Jackson and told him Ellen was there and needed a couple of men to help unload the car. Chad, Davis and Jackson came in to help.

"I'll get George and go out to the barn for the tree. It will take the two of us to get it in the stand. The chores are done so we are yours to help where you need us."

Chad and Davis unloaded her car while Jackson and George got the tree. Ellen loved it. She told them she would need a tall ladder to decorate it. The ceilings in the house were 10 feet and the tree almost reached it.

Joyce brought them donuts and coffee. She asked what she could do to help. Ellen gave them all a job and everyone got to work decorating.

"Barbara, I will bring the plants and flowers on Friday. Everything will be ready then. The house will be ready for the wedding. It is going to be beautiful."

"Ellen, I can't thank you enough. It would have been easier for you if I stayed with our original plan. I appreciate you doing this so much."

They worked for the next two days decorating the house for Christmas and the wedding. Everyone came to help at one time or another. It ended up being a family time of fun. Barbara realized she now had a wonderful and generous family.

They not only helped her, but they went to Cal's house and helped him and Gloria get their house decorated. They told them all it was their Christmas present, just a little early. It was their way of welcoming Gloria and Barbara to the family.

"Barb, we have planned your shower for Wednesday night. The men will just have to go out to dinner again. I told them not to get to use to it though."

"Thank you, Meredith you have all been so wonderful these last two weeks. I know we have put a lot on all of you by doing our weddings this way."

"We are all enjoying it. This is what families do for each other. You are both a part of our family. You don't have to be blood related to be family. We are a witness to the fact. Our Mom and Dad were the best parents any children could have had. They loved us as much as they would have if we were born to them."

"I know, Jackson talks so fondly of them. He loves all of you so much. I have come to love you all very much. Thank you for making me welcome. God is so good to his children."

The house looked so beautiful. Wednesday, Ellen brought in some flowers and plants for the shower. She told Barbara she would take them back to the shop until Friday. She wanted to keep them fresh.

The women showed up for the shower and the men left for the restaurant. They had a wonderful time. Barbara couldn't believe all the wonderful gifts she got.

When the men came back, they all came in to look at the gifts and to get their wives.

Hank and Anna told them they were so happy for them. They would see them Friday night for the rehearsal dinner. They needed to get home and check on their children.

Barbara gave them a hug and told them thank you. Jackson gave Anna a hug and shook hands with Hank. They said their good byes and left.

Tom told Rand and Ramona the deed for their ranch was ready. He said the rancher was going to be in his office at nine in the morning to finalize the sale. Rand told him they would be there. He has the check ready for him.

"Jackson, we will leave for Tennessee right after your wedding. We will need to pack up our things and get them moved here to the ranch. Tom says we will close at nine tomorrow morning. The rancher will be moving while we are gone. Could you have one of your ranch hands take care of the horses until we get back here?"

"It is no problem Rand; we will take care of them for you. Tell the rancher to call me when he is leaving and I will make sure they are taken care of."

When everyone had left, Rand and Ramona went up to their room. Jackson and Barbara went in his office to do their devotions and talk. They thanked God for everything he has done in their lives and for the great friends and family he has given them.

The next morning when Barbara and Jackson went to the kitchen the cleaning crew was there getting everything ready for the wedding. Jackson gave her a kiss and said he was getting impatient for Saturday to get there.

"Jackson, it won't be long now. I want to start moving some of my things to the house. I don't want to wait until the last minute. I need to get back to work on Monday. The others have taken care of my work long enough and they will have to do it again when we go on our honeymoon."

"Honey, bring over whatever you want. Your closet in the master bed room is empty and so is your dresser. I will help you when you are ready to bring them over."

Barbara spent most of the day Thursday packing up her things and cleaning the apartment for Joyce and George to move in. She put up a small tree and some decorations. They do so much for her. She wanted everything to look nice for them.

"Jackson, I have everything packed up. I only kept what I will need until the wedding. I will move the rest on Saturday morning".

"Joyce, I have the apartment ready so you can start moving in it. I just have some clothes and bathroom things to move on Saturday. I will give you a key and you can move whatever you want any time."

"We will probably move some things tonight. I have been packing things for a couple of weeks now. Thank you, it will make it a lot easier not having to move everything on Saturday along with everything else going on."

Friday morning Ellen came early to take care of the flowers and plants for the wedding.

"Ellen, everything is looking so beautiful. I can't believe how wonderful everything looks". She gave Ellen a hug and told her how much she loved it all.

Friday night everyone showed up for the dinner and rehearsal at Jeff and Lora's. Jeff said the blessing and asked God to bless their wedding and life together. Jackson gave his brother a hug and told him he loved him.

The rehearsal was fast they already knew what to do. It was just a formality.

"Barbara and Jackson, I am so happy for you both and I forgive you for not having me perform the wedding. It is nice to just enjoy everything for a change."

"Thank you, Pastor Nate. We are glad you are going to be able to enjoy yourself."

Barbara was up early on Saturday morning getting the rest of her things ready to go over to the house. She smiled when she thought about this being her wedding day. She wondered why she wasn't nervous. Meredith and she have to go to the beauty shop at one o'clock to get their hair done. She wanted to make sure she has everything done before then.

When she went to the house Jackson gave her a kiss. Honey you can put everything away you need too. I will stay out of your way today. I'm not suppose, to see you today but I had to give you a kiss."

He left and went out to the stable to help feed and then he was going over to Rand's ranch with him to check on the horses.

The rancher moved out on Friday so they needed to feed and turn the horses out to exercise. Rand would take care of them before he left tonight and Jackson would take care of them while he is gone.

Barbara and Meredith went to town for their hair appointment. The wedding was at four o'clock. They wanted it to be early so Cal and Barbara could leave for their honeymoon and Rand and Ramona could leave for Tennessee.

Cal and Gloria were taking the motorhome. Jackson had it detailed and serviced for them. He made sure there was a full tank of diesel fuel in it.

When they got to the house, Ellen had taken care of the flowers and plants. Everything looked so beautiful, Barbara had tears in her eyes.

They went up to the extra master suite to dress and do their makeup. Ellen came in with their bouquets.

"Ellen the bouquets are beautiful." They were red and white.

"Barbara, you are a beautiful bride. Jackson is going to die when he sees you."

Jasper came in to see if she was ready. She gave him a hug and told him thank you for giving her away. They heard the band start to play the songs before the wedding song. They were not using the traditional wedding march. The song they picked was a beautiful gospel song they love.

When they got to the top of the stairs Meredith started down. When she was half way down the band started playing the song they picked and Barbara on Jasper's arm walked down the stairs. When Jackson saw her his heart stopped for a second. This beautiful woman was marrying him. He couldn't take his eyes off her. His brother poked him and told him to breath.

When she got to him, Jasper handed her over to Jackson and told him to take good care of her. She gave him a kiss on his check and he had tears in his eyes.

When they stood before Jeff, he started the ceremony. He said he was honored to be marrying his brother to this wonderful woman. When he got to their vows, he announced they were saying their own vows to each other.

"Barbara, I have waited five years for this day. God had his plan for us. I have loved you all this time and will love and cherish you for the rest of my life. We will always keep God in our lives and home."

"Jackson, I fell in love with you when I was 17 years old. God knew we belonged together, but it wasn't time. He brought us together again with a stronger faith and love. I will love you forever. God will always be a part of our lives. You are in my heart forever."

"By the power invested in me by the state of Virginia and God, I now pronounce you husband and wife. You may now kiss your bride. I now give you Mr. and Mrs. Jackson Barnes."

When they went in to cut the cake, Jackson and Barb gave Cal and Gloria a hug and told them to get out of there and go on their honeymoon. Jackson gave Cal the keys to the motorhome and thanked them for everything.

Rand and Ramona came over to wish them well and congratulate them. They said they would be back in a few days.

"Jackson, I will call when we are on our way back."

"Rand, drive careful and we will see to the horses while you are gone."

They enjoyed the reception.

"Barb, I have looked forward to dancing with my bride. Honey, I love You so much and will always love You.

"I feel the same way about you my darling."

"It is kind of nice to not be rushing away. I am glad Cal and Gloria are on their way. She said they would be gone for two weeks. She didn't want to leave Mitch any longer. Cal wanted to take him, but she said no. They need this time alone. She is right, they have postponed their honeymoon long enough. They can take Mitch on a family vacation this summer."

"Well darling now, we have to get through Meredith and Brad's wedding. I wonder what is going on with Pat and Beth. I thought they would be talking about marriage by now."

"Sweetheart, I love you. Now we are married you think everyone should be. If God has plans for them to be together, they will be. He is more than capable of handling it."

"You are right my darling. What do you say we get out of here? I think everyone can handle it without us."

Jackson had planned a surprise for Barbara. He took her out to the car and she saw a suitcase in the back seat.

"We are going to a hotel for the weekend. Everything is taken care of here. We will be back on Monday morning. I love you my wife."

Dear Readers,

I hope you have enjoyed your visit in Hidden Valley with Jackson and Barbara. They have enjoyed having you visit them.

God had plans for their lives even though it took them a while to find their way. They appreciate you coming along with them as they found God's plan for them.

The Hidden Valley Youth Ranch has a lot of wonderful things in store for the youth of the area. It is making a difference in the lives of these young people.

Please come back and visit us again. You will not be disappointed in what God has in store for the people of Hidden Valley and you. A place where you can find good people who love each other and God.

God Bless you all,

Penny Heggie Austin